Dark Secret

Dark Desires

Book 3

Summer Cooper

D1521515

Lovy Books

Chapter 1
Emily

I had to live my life. My brother could take a long walk off a short pier if he thought he could control me with threats. I was the master of my fate, not him—not anybody else.

Even if my life had just been turned upside down and I was left alone again. I'd chosen to tell my brother to back off when he'd found out I was seeing Dylan James. Unfortunately, I'd just walked out on Dylan. I didn't want to sign another one of his contracts, so I'd left him in his apartment. I'd made the choice to tell Dylan he could shove his contract. Okay, so I'd hoped he'd follow me out and proclaim his undying love. Well, maybe not all that, but an agreement to not have a contract would have been nice.

It seemed I'd made this lonely, empty bed I'd just woken up in. I'd only been able to sleep a few hours off and on throughout the night. My brain kept waking up and replaying the words I'd had spoken with Dylan. I'd go to sleep for an hour, and then I'd wake up to remember every sentence that was said between myself and Trent.

I was exhausted from my attempts at sleep, but hopeful that someone had contacted me. I dragged my phone over to lay it below my pillow so I could see if the light was blinking. It always blinked when I had a message or voicemail.

I stared at the dark screen of my phone: no texts messages, no missed calls, it was just blank. Nobody wanted to talk to me because I'd chosen to live my life how I wanted to. I was paying the price for that rebellion now.

My head started to pound, and I curled up around the extra pillows on my bed. When would this nightmare end? Alright, it had only been a few hours since all of this happened, but somebody could have contacted me. Roxie, or, well, she was about the only one who might have.

Trent and Dylan may hate each other, but I could guarantee you they were thinking the same thing right now. I could just imagine them both, sulking and having a bit of a temper tantrum, while I was here alone with nobody to talk to now. Dylan could talk to his mother, or his father now that the man was better and on the mend. Trent had Jess, or his children, our brothers, or our mother and father to talk to.

According to Trent, they were all off limits to me now. Even my nieces and nephews. What a mess this all was. I rolled over, but that only made my head pound even more. This was not how I'd planned to spend the rest of my life. Of course, I'd not really had a plan, other than get rid of my virginity, experience some real sex, and find out what life had to offer.

I rolled out of bed, took a shower that partially relieved my headache, and then had some orange juice while two pieces of bread toasted in the toaster. The juice seemed to clear the rest of the headache away, and I was left with possibilities. I reached for a notebook I'd left on the table in the kitchen and grabbed a pen.

I wrote the words 'My New Life' at the top and started to put numbers in. I added a few lines into the list as I munched on the toast but soon came up short. I'd written down new haircut and new clothes, but I'd already started on the second one. I had a new home of my own, and a car, my own income, and I didn't have to work.

I could do whatever I wanted to do. But what did I want to do? I'd wanted to help my brothers run the hotel and had finished a degree in that field. Now, it seemed pointless. I could go to work for other hotels, but would they hire a Thompson? I bit at the inside of my cheek as I pondered and tapped the end of the pen against my notebook.

Would anybody want someone who could very well be a spy in their midst? Would they be too afraid my loyalties would lie with my family and keep me in low positions where inside information would be kept from me? What else could I do with my degree?

I wasn't sure, so I put that down on the list. Find out what I could do besides hotel management. Why? My brain eventually protested. I didn't need to work.

I looked around the house and knew I had to have something to keep me busy. The charity I volunteered at with Roxie wasn't doing a lot lately, and we had nothing planned for the future either. Maybe I should organize a fundraiser or something? I marked it down as a possibility.

Perhaps I could volunteer at another charity? Or take up a new hobby?

My phone buzzed, and I hated to admit it, but I nearly broke it as I tried to pick it up, and it went flying off the table. I finally got it in my hand and swiped without even looking who it was. Was it Trent? Dylan? Roxie? Jesse maybe?

"Hi, Emily? This is Debra down at Happy Nails. You have in an appointment in half an hour; we just wanted to remind you."

"OH? Do I? I'll be right down then." It wasn't anyone I'd hoped for, but getting my nails done would be a distraction.

I threw on some clothes, just a pair of skinny jeans and a long, slouchy sweater in baby pink, and a pair of ankle boots in black leather. I looked shabby chic and left the house without a backward glance.

I might be a lonely girl, but I'd find a way to fill my time. I arrived at the nail salon early and looked around. I had two colors picked out by the time Debra came to get me.

"You ready, Emily?" She asked as I sat.

"Yes, I've picked these two out; could you do something with that?"

I'd been going to Debra for years, and she looked at me now with confusion.

"Are you sure you meant to pick up those colors?" She looked down at the pearly midnight blue powder polish and the neon green and blinked.

I'd never picked out such gaudy colors before, I was usually a French manicure kind of girl, or I'd go for a demure pink or nude color, but this was bright and would catch attention. I wanted something pretty, to make me feel pretty, and I knew she'd come up with a design that would amaze me.

"I'm turning over a new leaf," I proclaimed and waved my hands down my slouchy attire. "No more always serious, business-ready Emily for me. From now on, it's pretty, fun, and maybe just a little loud."

I gave her a wink and a smile, and she got to work prepping my nails. "Anything you want, Emily. I aim to please."

I watched as she took the old gel polish off, trimmed, shaped, and buffed my nails, and then, finally, delicately polished each nail with precision. She did a diagonal line on several fingers, a vertical line on two, and painted one blue and then used a white and green to make flower petals on one finger of each hand. Some glossy gel polish and the manicure was done.

I looked down at the chaotic, but absolutely beautiful colors that she'd given me and grinned. "Perfect. I'll be looking at these all day."

"I bet you will," Debra agreed and took her mask off. We finished up the business of payment, and soon I was on my way.

I knew I was just avoiding going home. I loved that place, and still did, but damn, it was big and empty with just me there. I didn't like the way sound echoed back. Maybe I needed more furniture? Pillows and stuff like that. Big rooms always sounded emptier when there wasn't a lot of clutter in them to dampen the sound.

I headed to the nearest mall and bought even more stuff to put around the house. Candles, candle holders, giant vases full of faux plant life, wall hangings, little chairs that would never hold the average American but would fill space, and even several sets of beer crates. They would hold … stuff. I didn't know what, but I'd find something to put in them.

I headed home with my new household junk, and it took me four trips to empty out the car, but I didn't care. It was eating up the minutes that I was alone. Another hour saw the house a little more decorated, but still silent. It also kind of looked like I'd gone crazy at a yard sale, but I didn't care. The house didn't feel as empty now.

That was the crux of the problem. My phone hadn't beeped or buzzed all day long. I checked it quite often. Far more than I cared to admit. I was a sad case, but this was just pitiful. I didn't even have business contacts to call me.

For a minute, I thought about calling Jessi just to see if she'd answer. I talked myself out of it and scrolled through my contacts. Dylan's name was there at the top, an A in front of his name to make sure of that. My fingers hovered, and then finally I clicked on it. I'd send him a text message.

I composed a dozen different lines but deleted each one. He didn't deserve me. Not if he couldn't take me without a contract, or at the very least, explain to me why he so desperately needed a contract. I knew the stories of men who had been taken to the cleaners, but in the majority of cases, things like being sued didn't happen.

For that matter, he should've known by now that I wasn't like whoever the woman was who gave him such a complex. I wasn't about to kid myself and pretend that this need for a contract was normal. I saw it as childish, but I also knew it was some deep part of his psyche, something in him that would not allow him to relax without that piece of paper to reassure him.

It was like women who wouldn't have sex without marriage first. Did they really think that would stop a man from sleeping with another woman? Or that the marriage would last forever? Okay, maybe that was a bit snide of me to think like that, but really? What did people think a piece of paper could really do?

It was what the promise on that piece of paper said that mattered. As far as this ridiculous contract went, it held no water at all legally. A promise, as far as I was concerned, meant far more to me because I had a little bit of integrity. I didn't like going back on my word, and if I said I'd do something, then I'd do it. Barring unforeseen circumstances, of course.

Sometimes you just couldn't get to a charity function if you were too busy being sick from a stomach bug you picked up from your niece or nephew. Otherwise, I did as I said I would.

So why Dylan felt this was necessary really got to me, you would think by now I'd proven myself to him. He'd done things to me, seen parts of me; seen me in situations that I'd never allowed another human being to experience. Didn't that deserve some kind of trust? That was what it had boiled down to, really. He didn't trust me. Or was it himself?

Now, where had that thought come from? I went to the fridge, poured myself a glass of wine, and came back to the couch. Was he afraid of himself maybe? Did he think that piece of paper would put a shield around him and prevent him from developing feelings for me? Was that it? If that was the case, he failed already.

The man had said from day one that he didn't want a relationship. He'd asked me for a contract for a few days, then a couple of weeks, and now, he wanted another one? As I pointed out to him last night, we were already in a relationship by now. That brick wall he'd built with his contract hadn't worked this time.

Maybe that was really the problem? He knew I'd already gotten under his skin, and that made me pause with the glass halfway to my mouth.

Dylan had feelings for me. Shit.

I blinked and then chugged my wine down.

It was so obvious, wasn't it? Why hadn't it dawned on me until now?

It hadn't stopped him from asking for that contract, though. Would his feelings win out over his head now? Maybe?

I couldn't swear that; I didn't want a lifetime of what Dylan gave me. So far, he made me feel like I was perfect, as if no other woman could make him as happy as I did. If I was honest, I doubted anyone could make me as happy as he'd made me. I loved being with him, whether that was during sex, when we slept together peacefully, or when we were watching films.

I remembered our trip to the island and thought that might have been the most perfect time we'd had so far. I wanted more days like that, days when we were almost a normal couple. Days when I could care for him as more than just my sir. I wanted to rub his feet when he'd come home from work and to cook for him. I wanted to ease into long baths with him and wash the day away from his skin.

I wanted to hold him when he needed to be held and laugh with him when he needed that. Instead, I was alone on my couch, my pride intact, but my heart starting to crack. Trent had already broken it, but Dylan had put his own little crack there now.

I didn't know if I could stand this loneliness or the way everything had turned out. I'd given up my family for my pride. I wasn't even technically with Dylan, but I'd chosen him over my family. Well, that wasn't the whole of it.

They'd treated me like shit for ages now, and I'd basically dumped them because of it, but I would have gone back, eventually. If Trent hadn't come over here and shown his ass.

I wouldn't be disrespected in my own home by anybody, least of all my brother. I was paying the price for that pride, and before long, it might be me who cracked. I went for another glass of wine, the need to drown my sorrows strong now.

Chapter 2
Dylan

She'd left me, and it was a hard concept to swallow. And I really needed to swallow; my mouth was as dry as a desert. My brain quieted down once I put my head on the pillow, and my thoughts turned right to Stephanie. I'd never been left by a partner before. Ever. Our time together would end, and they would move on; well, most of the time it was me who moved on, but I'd never been walked out on.

I'd woken up with a hangover of epic proportions, and the words *she walked out on me* banged in time with the pain that pulsed in my head. I rolled over in bed and stared at the window. How was it still dark outside? Surely the sun should have risen by now?

I flopped my hand around for my phone to see what time it was and blinded myself when the screen came on. The pain that lanced from my eyes into my brain was just one more thing telling me I'd had too much to drink last night.

It was seven pm. How the hell had that happened?

I went into the kitchen, where I'd left my laptop, and sure enough, the clock read 7:03. I'd scratched my head and tried to figure out how the fuck I'd slept the day away. I ignored the notifications of emails and messages on my laptop and phone and went into the bathroom. None of the attempts of contact were from Stephanie, so fuck it. I'd wanted a shower, a shave, and some kind of food.

And maybe a couple of aspirin with some

orange juice. The orange juice gave me pause when I saw it in the fridge. I'd never kept juices or healthy snacks in the house until Stephanie came into my world. Now it was routine to grab some juice or a banana instead of a soda or a bag of chips.

I'd picked up the banana on the counter, looked glumly at the brown spots, and ate it anyway. It might give the aspirin time to kick in before I got dressed to go out. There was no real food in the house, so I'd have to go out and find something somewhere.

I could always call for food to be delivered, but I needed to get out. The pain in my head made me restless, and I needed to distract myself. I drove to a diner close by and went in. The smell of cooking waffles made me sick to my stomach, but I knew I'd get used to it. I sat and ordered a steak and cheese sandwich with hash browns, and I stared out of the large pane of glass.

Cars with bright headlights whizzed by, and

I couldn't help but wonder where they were headed. It was something else Stephanie had taught me, curiosity about those around me. She was always wondering things like where the woman with the red bag and the bright yellow pants was off to in such a rush, or if the man with the sad face that kept staring at the same page of the paper needed someone to lend him a hand. She'd noticed things like that, and it was just one of the many endearing things about Stephanie.

Until I'd met her, people had either been in my way or on the peripheral and didn't matter. Now, I wondered if the man with the briefcase who sat in the booth ahead of me was a banker, a drug dealer, or a doctor without a family to go home to.

She'd already changed me, and I'd barely spent any real time with her. We'd spent a lot of time having sex and going out, but that still wasn't quality time. Not like my parents' marriage.

My brain kind of froze at that point. My real parents. I'd tried to never think of them because it just brought back heartache for me. A flashed memory flitted through my mind. Mom as she screamed at Dad that she hated him. She always hated him when she was in that mood. The tears on her face as she screamed. The accusations she'd made that final night, her face as she left my room, just before the smell of gasoline hit me.

I'd learned to fear my mother long before that moment, and something had told me to get out of the house. I'd climbed out of the window and tried to find my dad. I'd thought he had been in his shed in our back yard, toddling around with his HAM radio stuff, but he hadn't been there. As flames flickered in the dark windows, it had hit me that Dad must have been in the house still. I'd tried to get back in, but the house had lit up like a bomb had gone off inside.

I didn't know how much gasoline Mom had

used, but it was a lot. Once the fire was out, and I'd been told both of my parents were dead, came even more chaos. I'd been arrested for arson. A thirteen-year-old kid with a reputation for being a loner, surly, and always in black, the cops had assumed I'd been the one to set it. Mom and Dad were found in bed together.

I'd protested, I'd begged anybody, somebody to listen to me. I'd been headed for a trial when forensic reports came back and showed Dad had died from a single gunshot wound to the head, long before the fire got to him. The gun was still in Mom's hand.

I tried to brush the memory away, to focus on the sandwich that was placed in front of me, but that night and the events that followed played on. Unstoppable.

Mom had always been a nutcase. She'd made sure she got pregnant with me to trap Dad into marriage, and that had eaten at her already unstable conscience. She was always accusing him of cheating, of things that made no sense, when all he did was work and come home to her. Even I knew Dad wasn't cheating, but she'd get in these moods, and there'd be this look in her eyes. A look that terrified me immensely, even when I was thirteen. She'd had that evil in her eyes all of that day, and I'd gone to bed early with a book to avoid her.

I'd woken up when she came in and brushed my hair from my face. "I've always loved you, baby boy. You gave me your father, but it's time now. It's time to end his infidelity and to make sure you never leave me either. Sleep well, my boy, Mommy loves you."

I'd kept my eyes shut and my breathing even up to that point. I'd pretended to be asleep as the sound of something splashing against the hardwood floor made my ears twitch. I'd looked up at her when I smelled the gasoline and caught her face in the moonlight. There'd been nothing but madness there.

Yes, she'd been insane, but her insanity

was her love. She'd felt that she'd trapped my father into marriage, and she'd gone crazy over it. My dad hadn't consented to the life she'd brought on him; she'd tricked him, and I was living proof of that trickery. She'd given him fourteen years of hell, and all he'd ever done was try to make her happy.

He'd never resented me, or the fact that I'd existed. He'd loved her, despite her mental illness. He'd loved her through countless episodes that ended with the house destroyed and her in a puddle on the floor in his arms. My father and I would clean the house up, and eventually, we stopped decorating the walls and the shelves. She couldn't throw what wasn't there.

It had all taken its toll, and on that one final night, she'd shown me exactly what consent meant. It meant I'd never had to live with insanity again. Because if you both knew what you were walking into, then there would be no doubts, right? No guilt. Or insanity.

So why couldn't Stephanie understand that? It was simple, really, and perhaps it seemed trivial to her, but it wasn't a laughing matter. You had to know exactly what you were getting into, and for me, that was sex that could sometimes stray from the bedroom with whips and chains attached. Other times, it meant I needed my solitude.

I didn't want a relationship because I doubted I'd ever been able to have what my adoptive parents had. I didn't exactly deserve a love like that. With my past, it wasn't hard to understand why I'd shy away from long-term relationships either. I was the reason my mother killed my father and then herself. The reason why she'd tried to erase my existence from the world.

I picked up my sandwich and bit into it, but I didn't taste it. I could tell it had gone cold, but I didn't care. The memories of my origins took the taste away, dulled my senses and my mind. I'd need a drink after this.

I finished my food off and went back to the penthouse. A swim might do me good. The exercise was nice, and the heated water soothed the aches, but it did little to soothe my mind. I heard my phone ringing and wanted it to be Stephanie so fucking bad.

It wasn't; it was my adoptive mother. I dried my hands and called her back since I'd missed the call.

"Hey, Mom, what's up?" I sat down on a lounger, the towel around my waist. There was something about talking to a parent that made me feel ashamed of swimming naked in my own pool.

"Hiya, son, you didn't call me yesterday, and I was worried. You always call me on Fridays."

"What? Today's Friday, Mom."

"No, it's not. That was yesterday, baby. Have you got your days mixed up?" She sounded concerned, but I reassured her with a chuckle.

"Silly me; you're right." Holy fuck, I'd lost two days, not just one? How much had I drunk? "Too much work distracting me."

"Well, you need to take a break then, son. Have a night off, and just relax." Mom's voice had lost the concerns and was now full of chiding. She was good at that, but it always came across as motherly, not nagging.

She was right, though. I needed to figure my life out. I'd drunk myself stupid for two days over a woman? Yeah, but Stephanie wasn't just any woman. She blew my mind in so many ways. In the bedroom, out of it, and it wasn't just her sexiness. She was intelligent, beautiful, and kind. To me, with me, and to others. She was just … different and sweet.

Maybe this was all wrong of me. Maybe I needed to start acting like I wasn't damaged goods. This woman that I definitely didn't deserve wanted me, on her own terms. Could I do that?

Could I trust a woman without a contract

guiding what happened or didn't? All bets would be off. She'd be able to walk away when she wanted to, if I actually went into a relationship with her. I felt confused, and that frustrated me to no end.

I knew by now that no other woman would do for me. I'd tried to have a little fun one night when I first met her, and I hadn't been able to get her off of my mind. I'd gone home, instead, and that should have been the first warning that something wasn't right. That she'd already started to change me.

Stephanie, with those tempting gray eyes and that infectious laugh of hers. Could I go on much longer without her? I doubted it if I'd had to sleep two days to get over the shock of her walking out on me. How did I go about this while keeping some of my pride intact?

I left the pool room and moved into the dark living room. I went to the glass walls to stare out at the city below. Cars and resort hotels turned the darkness into day in the distance, but from my lofty perch I could see darkness that reigned on the outskirts. That was kind of like me with Stephanie.

At the center was fun, life, light, and on the outskirts? Dark emptiness. She'd brought so much to me, and one of those things was this feeling I'd tried to ignore, up until she'd tore up the contract and walked out on me. Completion. I didn't feel so … *hollow*, inside anymore. Not when she was around.

I'd seen the hurt and anger in her eyes and ignored it that night. I'd thought my will was stronger, and she'd bow down, in true sub fashion, and give in to my demands for a signed contract. Instead, she'd shown a subs prerogative and walked out. She'd shown some sense, in fact. She'd been right about one thing —signing contracts so frequently was stupid.

Maybe, just maybe, I could offer her one for six months. Would that be long enough to get her out of my system? Would that be long enough for her to grow tired of me?

This time it was me who chewed at their lip. I swiped my hand over my jaw and thought about it. Could I go to her and be with her? Without a contract? That was scary to me. Dangerous even. I didn't want a relationship, but little Miss Stephanie had changed all of that.

I was fairly certain I'd wanted a relationship with her. My heart raced, and my blood heated as I thought about a little more than just sex and someone to watch a movie with. A woman to maybe, care for? I wasn't about to say love because that was just a stupid concept women made up, but caring and friendship were real.

Would she want me to call her? Should I go to her house and ask for forgiveness? It had been two days. She was probably fuming by now and ready to throw her shoes at me. She had a pretty good collection of those, I'd noticed. Some of them were rather pointy too. Hmm.

I'd tried to call her, but the call went right to

voicemail. She was either screening her calls or the phone was off. As I knew she'd never turned her phone off, it must have been that she didn't want to talk to me. Well then.

Maybe a drive to see Roxie and get her opinion on all of this, was in order.

Chapter 3
Emily

The thing about having stuff in your house to dampen the echo was that it needed to be cleaned. I'd barely had my new knickknacks for a week and dust had already started to settle on all of them. I probably wouldn't have noticed two weeks ago, but as I looked around the house for something to fill my time, the first signs of dust caught my eye.

I'd found a dusting cloth and some utensil I'd bought because it promised to cut my cleaning time in half and headed to the living room first. I polished the candle holders and dusted the beer crates I'd moved in from the hallway. They looked cute in there, but boy, did they collect dust. Then I'd made my way through the rest of the house and polished up a few more things, and before I knew it, I was on my hands and knees, cleaning the grout in the bathroom. This was not how I'd planned to spend my day, but then I didn't really have a plan.

I threw off the yellow plastic gloves I'd put on to protect my nails and skin and looked around. I was lonely, but I was also a little upset. I thought Dylan would have called me by now. He hadn't, though, and that made me angry. Well, more hurt than angry, but still. He could have at least sent me a message or something.

I didn't think he was serious when he'd said it was over if I left. People said things like that all the time, but they didn't mean it. I'd figured he'd be angry for a little while, and then he'd come around and see me, his face sheepish. Or

I'd get a message asking if I wanted to go and eat. There'd been none of that.

I'd twisted my mouth around as I thought about spending the rest of my evening on my hands and knees, but this time scrubbing instead of, well … those other things. Oh, those things I was starting to miss really badly. I sat back against the wall and thought about the things I'd done with Dylan and wondered.

Hmmm.

Could I? No, I couldn't. Maybe, if it was someone similar… I didn't think I could do any of that kind of stuff with someone who wasn't Dylan, but I wouldn't know until I tried, would I? It had been a week since I'd left his place. There'd been no communication. Maybe it really was over?

If that was the case, there was no use in sitting here, waiting on a call that wouldn't come. I got up, took a shower, dressed up a little, put my now well-worn mask in my bag, and headed for Elmo's. I'd have a drink or two, have a look around, and see what happened. Surely, Dylan wouldn't be there? Maybe he'd found a property by now and was planning to move on, his conquest in the bag.

He knew Roxie and I were friends, and that I might turn up there. He wouldn't dare come in, not if he wasn't looking for me. I went in the back way, my mask in place from the moment I'd parked the car, and found Roxie quickly. She'd just finished her set and was in her dressing room, about to change her clothes after a quick shower.

She'd hugged me, before she sat down, her dressing gown a whirl of purple silk around her. "Tell me, baby."

"Well, I needed some time out of that house. I feel like a ghost in it sometimes. Like I'm haunting it or something."

"Oh, don't be ridiculous. Has Dylan called?" Her pretty face, heavily made up but artfully so, examined my features, and didn't find a hint of sadness. I'd done my makeup well and hidden the dark circles under my eyes.

"No, and at this point, I don't care if he calls." I schooled my features into a defiant look, flipped my blonde hair out of my face, and stared off into the distance. "He can just fuck right off."

"Do you mean that, though?" she asked as she put a pencil skirt on over a pair of lacy panties and a very supportive bra. She'd slid a matching top on with a peplum waist and a plunging neckline. The deep burgundy color suited her, and I'd wondered how the same outfit would look on me.

I looked down at the black silk dress that barely covered my thighs, and knew I was elegantly dressed, but that was sexy and smart looking. I'd decided to order some more clothes when I got home.

"Emily!" she whispered loudly and bent down to look me in the eyes. Blue met gray, and I backed my head up to avoid her.

"Of course, I mean it. He hasn't called; he hasn't been by..." I didn't finish because she pulled on a pair of shoes and sat beside me.

"You aren't here looking for someone to replace him with, are you? Or, heaven help me, make him jealous if he finds out?" Again, she leaned into me and looked deep into my eyes.

"I'd kind of..." I let the words trail off because I felt guilty. That was basically my plan, even if I didn't want to admit it. "Too dramatic?"

"Girl, if I could count how many times women have done that and regretted it. I don't recommend it, though, others might. You'll just end up feeling trashy, and it won't solve anything. If you want him, then you'll just have to wait. Instead, come have a drink with me and don't do something you'll regret."

"Is that what you did when Freddy didn't renew your contract?" I asked softly, because I didn't want to hurt her, but I also wanted to know. We headed to the bar as Roxie answered.

"I drank myself silly the first night, at home, where nobody had to pick up the pieces. Then, I went back to work. I've got another fella on the line already, though. Freddy's moved on, and I have to face that."

"You just said I shouldn't do that." I was confused, and my face showed it. The barman brought us our drinks, and we went to a table.

"Do what?" She looked equally confused as we sat.

"Replace him with another man."

"Oh, honey, no." She laughed. "Mine is strictly business. That's different. No man will ever hold my heart. There isn't one man enough for the challenge."

I knew she'd meant it, and I'd wondered, not for the first time, exactly what she'd lived through in her life. Roxie's practicality was always something I'd admired, and it didn't surprise me that she'd face hurt with the same attitude. You couldn't change someone's mind, even if you'd wanted to, and business was business. I saw the sense of her words, and knew I'd been right to come to her. She took my hand, purely platonically, and looked at me with renewed curiosity.

"Do you love him? Is that the problem?" She didn't chew at her lip, but I knew she'd wanted to by the way her lips pursed.

"I don't think I know him enough to love him, Roxie." I looked away, completely surprised at this sudden intimacy.

"Have you ever, ahem, have you ever been in love before, Em, ah, Stephanie?" She didn't look at me until she almost used my real name.

I stared back at her, certain I looked like a deer caught in the headlights, even behind my mask. How did I answer that? I'd never had time. I'd gone to an all-girls school, and I'd always been book-ended by a brother, a mother, my father or Jesse. I'd never had a moment alone to fall in love, much less be in love.

"No," I finally answered her.

"Ah, so that complicates it even more, then." She looked away and pursed her lips again, her eyes narrowed. "Hmmm."

It seemed I wasn't the only one doing that lately, then. "Well?"

"I don't know. Perhaps..." She paused and looked deeper at me, although I'd been certain that was impossible a second ago, but she managed to do it now. "You know, I wouldn't say this normally, but you know you weren't a very good sub, if you walked out on him."

I stared at her, shocked. My jaw even hung open a little bit as I stared back at her. "Not a very good ... I just ... well..."

"You can sit there and blink all you want to, my dear, but you weren't."

"He wanted another contract. I'm sick of signing contracts. He either wants me or he doesn't." I felt as if I'd been filled with some kind of righteous, burning light as I sat there, indignant. Not a very good sub, my ass!

"I don't know a lot about what goes on between you two, you're both very closed-mouth on the subject, but I think you're new to this and still learning. You can be forgiven for walking out on your dom. I could be wrong, but I think he's different with you. I don't know him very well, quite frankly, but from what you've said, he doesn't have a very tight leash on you. Something tells me that's not normal for him, though?" Her fingers tapped on the table, and she took on a faraway look.

"I can't wait for what you decide on next..." It dripped with sarcasm, but I didn't leave. Maybe she was right.

In the videos, and the vignettes I'd seen in the clubs, the doms had been much rougher with their subs. Dylan was definitely controlling when we had sex, and he had demands, sometimes, but he'd never actually left me in a lot of physical pain.

"Do you like pain, Em, er, Stephanie?" She licked her lips before she added more. "I mean really like it?"

"I, well, Dylan hasn't..." I stopped and licked my suddenly hot lips. This was definitely personal. "Uh."

"If you want my help, you have to talk to me."

"I'm not used to having such intimate conversations, that's all." I pulled away to ease some of the too intimate atmosphere. I couldn't talk to her while she held my hands. "It's just, I don't know what I want. I don't want to be degraded, not like some of those people in the videos..."

"That's fine. I think what you're after is more of a *safe* kind of experience. You're more of a brat who pushes her dom, if I was to guess."

"I suppose." Once she'd said it, the word kind of made sense. I wanted to be bad, to goad him into punishing me, in very sexy ways, not in the make me never act like that again, kind of way. "Yeah, that makes sense."

"So then, walking out is more of a tantrum for attention?" she supplied with a raised eyebrow.

"No. I'm sick of that shit." The words flew out, and there was no way to pull them back. I decided not to backtrack, simply because it was the truth.

"Okay. Would you, perhaps, be open to a longer one then?" Her dark eyebrow lifted over a glittering eye, and I couldn't help but frown.

"I'm sick of those, Roxie. Why can't he just take me as I am?"

"Because not everyone can trust like you can, Steph." At least she got the name right this time.

"You think he has trust issues?" I had kind of thought that but wasn't sure.

"He might. Most men do that insist on contracts." She sighed deeply and looked at me with a lot of concern. "Are you ready to face him?"

I turned my head, something in the tone of her voice told me. Or maybe it was the way my skin tightened, I didn't know, but I did know it ended with me staring right at him, at the bar.

Our eyes locked, and heartbreak filled me when he turned away. "Damn."

Roxie patted my hand and ordered me another drink.

"He's leaving," I whispered, the heartbreak hard to hide now.

"Maybe it's for the best, hun," Roxie whispered, but I knew she was wrong.

Dylan was meant for me. No matter what hurt in his past had made him need to be the one in control, no matter if he needed a contract or not. I remembered that weekend on the island all over again, and how I'd longed to be his forever. How I'd started to daydream about the future.

I wasn't sure I could ever have that with Dylan, but if I threw it away now, I'd never know would I? Besides, I'd chosen him over my family; I had to make it worth it, somehow.

Chapter 4
Dylan

I walked into the club, the plan to just have a drink, sit for a little while, maybe have a chat with Roxie, and then go home. I'd come in through the back way, but she hadn't been in her dressing room. Seeing Stephanie sitting there at a table with her was the last thing I'd expected.

She'd come here to find a dom, she'd walked out on me, so it made sense that she was on the hunt for a new one now. That thought kicked me in the guts, and when she turned and our eyes caught, well, I was certain my organs twisted into knots, not just my stomach.

I saw her hurt there, her questions, but I couldn't get myself to go to her. Because I'd also seen that little flash of defiance. She was still determined to not have a contract. Fuck it. I headed down to the lower levels of the club. If little Miss Thing wanted to have her way, then I'd let her. I wasn't going to give in, not now.

I took the elevator down to the playground as I'd come to think of it. I'd found an empty bedroom next to a room where two women were taking out the day's frustrations on a man. He was strapped to a low table, a ball gag in his mouth. His eyes were covered with a black strip of leather, and his ears were plugged. He could only smell and feel, maybe taste if they decided to use his mouth. I knew the table could be moved to make access easier.

Normally, this sort of thing didn't interest me, but I'd been wondering what Stephanie might do if our roles were reversed. I could definitely see her in the role of a dom, if she'd ever wanted to switch out. Not with me, I'd never let anyone have that kind of control of me, but she might enjoy the things the women were doing.

They had the man excited, I could see that, but I'd doubted they even really saw him as a real person in that moment. He was a penis, a mouth, an instrument to be used for their enjoyment. Stephanie might enjoy doing that to someone, to take away even their identity, but I wasn't sure she'd like being the one strapped down so much.

But, maybe, she'd like a taste of it. If I could figure out how to end this mess. She was only a few feet above my head, just right there. Within reach for the first time in a week. She'd looked delicious too, in that black dress that fit her frame so well. It had shown off her breasts.

I sank to the edge of the bed, hard as a rock at the mere thought of the weight of her silky flesh in my hands. I cupped my erection through my pants, but that didn't ease the ache there. It had only made it worse.

I'd took a deep breath and refocused on the trio across from me. They couldn't see me, but I could see them, and they knew it. There would have been a small green light that turned on at the top of ceiling the moment I locked the door to this room. They knew there was an audience watching.

One of them was a redhead, the other had naturally black hair. Both were attractive, but they weren't Stephanie. Still, I'd sat there and waited. I'd wanted her to come down to me, to watch this rather erotic, provoking display. I'd wanted to put her on her hands and knees and take her until I was satisfied. Then, I'd leave her to want more. There would be no satisfaction for her, as there wouldn't be for the fellow across the room from me.

That would be her punishment, I'd decided. She'd have to take what I gave her and no more. Then maybe she'd learn a lesson. I wasn't a brutal dom, after all. I wouldn't beat her because I had no desire to see dark purple bruises on her skin. It was too perfect to mar like that. Besides, I didn't want to inflict that kind of punishment on her. That kind broke the will and the spirit. I didn't want to take that from her.

I loved that aspect of her personality, of who she was. She had a mind of her own, and it was one of the things that I found the most attractive about her. There were many, many things about her to be enamored with.

How did I get her back, though? Roxie had told me yesterday that she didn't know how to get Stephanie to sign another contract. I'd felt like an idiot asking the other woman what to do, but I knew I could trust her. She'd approach it with her analytical mind and find a solution. I'd wondered if that was why Stephanie was here, some ploy of Roxie's, maybe.

Had she called Stephanie here to bring us together? If that was her plan, then it didn't work because Stephanie didn't run up to me and declare her undying commitment. She didn't make a single move; she just sat there and stared, and then I walked away. I'd been stunned to see her, so I walked away.

I banged my fist down on the bed, frustrated and angry that I couldn't come up with a solution to the whole thing. My pride wouldn't let me go to her, and she hadn't broken. I'd almost gone to her on more than one occasion. I'd even got in the car and drove in the direction of her house, but the last minute I'd changed my mind and turned around. I'd go back to my chair and do some more work.

Work had got me through this whole mess, and now that the deal that I'd managed to set up on the property had started to move along, there was even more work to do. Since my family owned a number of hotels, I had staff to do most of the work, but there was still a lot for me to do. I'd already started to work the numbers for renovating the resort. It hadn't been empty for long, but we'd want it to look like our brand. That meant a lot of redecorating had to be done and work orders had to be sent out.

Sure, I could let someone else do all of that, but I'd wanted this to be perfect. I had learned not to get too excited, Trent Thompson had a knack for jerking deals right out of my hands, but I had a feeling about this one. The owner hadn't listed the property yet when my real estate agent contacted them, and I was almost certain this was the one.

Even more frustrated now, I got up and left the room. There was nothing for me here, not without Stephanie. I headed out of the club, went home, and filled up a glass with scotch. I needed relief, but I hadn't found it at Elmo's. I had found Stephanie, however, and she was part of the problem. She was in my dreams, and in my thoughts, and it didn't matter how many times I took matters into my own hand, I couldn't get her out of my mind.

Even when I'd tried to work, she was in my head. I'd wanted to take her to the other hotels we had, show her what it was I'd worked so hard for. I'd wanted to take her up in the mountains in California and show her the sights, and to take her to the ski slopes in Colorado. I'd hated going home to Kansas, but I'd also wanted to take her there and show her where I'd grown up.

I'd wanted her by my side as I got this new resort off the ground. This was a test for my family and me, in many ways. We had a lot of hotels, that was for sure, but this would be my contribution to the chain. To our family's legacy. Although, that wasn't something I'd really thought about. A legacy.

As I'd settled into a chair at the kitchen table, my work spread out all around me, I'd thought about it. I had no children, and the couple who adopted me had no other children. Who would this empire I was trying to add to go to if something happened to me? When something happened to me?

I wasn't sure, and that bothered me. I'd never really wanted children before, not after my childhood, but the thought hit me and weighed on me heavily. Why was I was working so hard if there was nobody to leave all of this to? Even Trent Thompson had children, as did his brothers. There was a whole slew of inheritors there, but my family? There'd only been me.

Then my brain decided to really fuck me over and put the image of Stephanie with a baby in her arms into my mind. Something in my lower abdomen clutched, and my heart pounded. Fuck, what the hell was wrong with me?

I got up from the table and slugged down the scotch. I'd had plenty of years to worry about that, and if it came down to it, I could hire a surrogate, if need be. Marriage, romantic relationships, none of that was in my future. I'd laughed at myself for being so stupid. Hadn't my mother taught me anything?

Love made you crazy, and it made you do stupid shit, like murder the only man who had ever stuck by you. It made you stick by the woman who did nothing but hurt you and your child, over and over again, long after you should have had her put into care for her own safety. For your safety. If Dad had put mom in the hospital, he might still be alive, and that thought had burned through my soul for a long time now. He hadn't because he'd loved her. He thought he could love her back to sanity, but he hadn't been able to.

No amount of love would have done that, except that love that would have let her go to get help. Dad hadn't seen it that way, and he'd paid the ultimate price. I'd promised myself, all those years ago, that I would never fall victim to that kind of nonsense. The kind that could get you killed.

Maybe I should just walk away from all of

this, I'd thought for the first time. Leave the idea of a resort on the east coast behind, or move to a different state and start my search over again. Find someone new to play with, someone who understood the game and treated it as such.

Someone who didn't have Stephanie's eyes that saw right through me. Or the mouth that I'd loved to kiss, the mouth that could bring so much pleasure. Fuck, I was hard again now.

I went into the shower and tried not to think about her. I'd tried to convince myself to just pack my shit up and go. Even when I'd got out and had dressed again, I still couldn't convince myself that it was a good idea. I'd spent a lot of resources here already, and it would be stupid to just throw all of that away.

That felt better than admitting that I couldn't give up on Stephanie, not yet. Blaming my reluctance on that meant I didn't have to admit that I'd wanted to drive to her house, walk through her front door, carry her to the bed, and make her scream my name as she'd raked my back for more.

I'd grabbed the keys to a new toy I'd bought and headed down to the parking garage. I'd seen the shop when I'd turned around from one of my many abandoned trips to Stephanie's place. A brand new motorcycle, with an amazing paint job and an engine loud enough to drown out my very thoughts. Painted in black and blue metallic fleck paint, the monster of a bike was slung low and had a v-twin engine that didn't want to stop.

I threw a leg over the bike, started her up, and headed out to the highway. A long ride had been the only thing that could soothe me lately. It had been a whim to buy the bike, I hadn't ridden one since I was in my early twenties, but I'd kept my license valid, and hadn't forgotten how to ride one. With the engine vibrating my lower extremities, I flew into the night, the helmet on my head protecting me from the wind. I was glad I'd put a leather jacket on before I left, but my legs were a little cold in jeans.

None of it had mattered, not when I was on that bike. I drove for an hour, until my hands were tired of gripping the accelerator, and stopped at a twenty-four-hour diner to grab a cup of coffee. Stephanie was still in my head, but I didn't feel quite as frustrated now.

I'd give her a few more days, I'd decided on the way back home, and if she hadn't come to me by then, I'd go somewhere else. I'd go back to Kansas, or maybe out to California. There were quite a few nice stretches of road out there to take the bike on. I could drive out to Las Vegas from there, check on the resort in the city that was never fully dark, and then head to Kansas.

I couldn't believe I'd forgotten how awesome it was to be on the back of motorcycle. I'd grown into the corporate life like I'd been born to it and had left the rebellion of my youth behind. Now, a little older and a little wiser, I knew this would be part of my life, and that I'd probably go back on my decision to give Stephanie a few more days.

She had infected me, somehow, the little witch. I couldn't get her out of my system, and even though her leaving me had angered me, deep down it was the fact that it had hurt that she'd left that really bothered me. I could accept that anger, but not the hurt. I could accept that I'd wanted her so that I could fuck her and spend time with her as a friend, but I could not, would not, accept that I wanted her for far more than that. Even if my brain and my heart constantly reminded me that I did.

I drove the bike hard, reached speeds that would probably earn me a speeding ticket if there were speed cameras on the highway, or if a cop clocked me. I didn't care at the moment. I'd pay to get out of the ticket because I'd felt as if I was being chased, hounded by my own thoughts. When I broke 100 mph, my concentration was on keeping the bike off the ground and my head on my shoulders. I couldn't think about Stephanie anymore because I was concentrating on my preventing my own death.

I slowed as I came to the exit that would lead me to my home, my heart racing and blood pounding in my veins. I felt each beat of my heart as a pulse as my blood shot through my body. Yes, I needed a lot more of this and less time sitting at home, mooning over a woman. My thoughts were clear by the time I pulled up into the parking garage.

I'd stopped the bike, locked it up for the night, and just sat there on it. My blood still raced through my veins, but I'd felt calmer, my brain was quiet for once. For the first time in a week, I'd smiled. That had been fun.

I'd scoffed at my own stupidity, but had to admit, the race against myself had done me some good. I'd locked my helmet up in one of the saddlebags and headed for the elevator. Maybe I could get some sleep now.

I'd leaned back against the wall of the elevator and breathed in deep. Peace was a good thing, and I'd thought about having a swim too, before I headed to bed. I'd neglected my workout sessions over the last few days, and a swim would get me back in the game. I had made up my mind to do just that when the elevator came to a stop and the doors opened wide.

Stephanie was there, without her mask, her hands wrung together as those beautiful eyes stared up at me with uncertainty. I stared at her for only a second before I had her against my door, our lips locked together in a frantic reunion.

Chapter 5
Emily

After I saw Dylan walk out of the bar, I'd made my excuses to Roxie, and left. The place felt stifling, and I couldn't sit there. I didn't know if he was still in the place, or if he'd left; all I knew was I couldn't sit there if he was.

When I'd first seen him, my impulse was to run away. Then, I'd wanted to go up and whack him one for not calling me. Then I'd wanted to cave in to his demands. I'd gone home and stared at the empty rooms. Frustration made me jittery, and that put me on edge. I went to my laptop and decided to play a game on Facebook, maybe find a new one to play.

I went up to the search bar within the application and was about to type in free games when my fingers found the D key instead. I went to erase the letters and typed Dylan's name in. Of course, he didn't have a Facebook, not that I could see. Oh, there were plenty of people with his name, but he didn't have a profile. That's when I got the bright idea to open a new page on my browser and type in his name, along with the state he was from. Kansas.

That brought up a bunch of stuff that wasn't what I was looking for, and then I saw it, on the second page. Reports about a fire, two deaths, and the suspect was the son. My blood ran cold as I opened the link to see a much younger Dylan on the screen. His name had been Dylan Matthews back then, but the news sources had tagged it with his adopted name. There were several pictures of a very young Dylan, and my heart lurched over each one. His demeanor was defiant as he was led away in handcuffs, but another picture showed what was really going on. A broken little boy whose parents had just died, with a grief-stricken face as the police car drove away.

I scrolled back and found more reports, how his mother had been the one to set the fire, and on one rather gory site, I found the details of how Dylan had lived his life. Apparently, the information came from a friend of Dylan's parents, but it didn't say who that person was. All I could think as I read this horrific account was why hadn't someone done something, anything, to prevent what had happened?

His mother had been the problem, not Dylan, and it made me even angrier at Trent that he'd told me Dylan had killed his parents. He must have seen both reports, as I had. How could he accuse Dylan of that, when it wasn't true? When the truth was even worse; his own mother had tried to kill him!

He'd never told me much about his private life, not really; although I thought he'd started to a few times. Something always held him back. The openness in his eyes would hide behind an invisible shutter, and the moment would pass. He'd change the subject, or kiss me instead of telling me whatever secrets he'd kept locked away, and what secrets he'd hidden indeed.

I'd read the personal accounts over and over again, the way his mom would just descend into a screaming fit of bitter tears as she accused his father of sleeping with their neighbor, or a woman at work, were heart-wrenching. I felt pity for them all, but especially for the child who had come of that initial union.

Dylan had lived his whole life knowing his mom had conceived him on purpose, just to get a husband. His father had been a hard-working man, and he'd been devoted to his wife. The personal accounts told how everyone who knew the family knew that Dylan's dad was faithful. He only ever went to work, and then he'd go straight home to cook dinner and clean the house up. He'd tried to give Dylan some semblance of stability, but most of the time, the home was dysfunctional.

I'd tried to imagine Dylan after he'd been released from the jail and taken into foster care. The poor child wasn't even allowed to attend the dual funeral. Tears slid from my eyes as I'd pictured him, alone, afraid, and in a new home with strange people. The James couple had taken him, had given him a home, and had obviously helped him get his life back on track.

This is the reason he'd wanted the contract so bad? His mother had tricked his father and then made all of their lives hell. It made sense to me now. If that was the reason for his insistence, however. I'd stared at the screen, re-reading words I'd already read a dozen times. Who was this family friend? Were they honest, could they be trusted? The site wasn't exactly high-end; it could have been the writer's fantasy about what had happened.

Another question I had was why Dylan had gone to foster care. Hadn't there been grandparents or aunts and uncles who could have taken him in? He must have felt completely abandoned, I'd decided as I stared at the pictures that were sprinkled all over the page. The final picture was one of him being taken away by his new adoptive parents. The website wished Dylan luck, but it hadn't been updated in at least ten years. There were other pages I could have looked at, even more gruesome tales of twisted love and burning hate, but I'd only clicked on it to learn about Dylan.

Murder sites weren't my thing, and I'd closed the browser and my laptop after a few minutes of staring off into space. Dylan had lived an incredibly tumultuous life until he was taken in by the James family. It was hardly any wonder at all that he'd wanted a contract now. That didn't mean I'd decided to give him one, though.

It just meant I had to help him work his way past the need for black and white promises. He had to learn to take me at face-value and to trust my word. Just as I'd trusted him. I went into my bedroom and pulled out some leisure-wear: a soft pair of velour pants in a bright peach color, with a matching jacket that would come off easily, but keep me warm on the drive over.

There was no doubt I'd go to him now. A man who had lived through that kind of trauma would have too much pride, or maybe not enough, to let his guard down, or to admit that he'd needed someone. Maybe it was just wishful thinking, he might turn me away at the door, but I wouldn't know unless I tried, would I?

I drove over carefully, determined to get there in one piece. I didn't want to rush over and end up in a tree or worse. I took my time, and when I'd pulled into the parking garage, I'd rushed to the elevators. I knew the passcode to get to his floor, I'd memorized it weeks ago, and punched it in and turned to watch the numbers above the door.

I'd deliberately kept my mind blank on the way over and did my best to concentrate on the road in front of me. That kept the doubts at bay, but that ride up the building almost broke me. What if he wasn't home? What if he was and refused to see me? The code still worked, so he'd either hoped I'd come to him and left it alone, or he'd forgotten to change it. Or maybe he'd thought I wouldn't have the gall to show up there?

I chewed at the inside of my lip and tried not to groan in misery. Surely, he'd be happy to see me? The thought occurred to me that he might still be at the club, already entangled with another woman, contract signed and delivered. That made me want to punch somebody's lights out, and I'd never been a violent person.

Even in school, I'd always stayed out of fights and arguments. I'd just hated the turmoil and drama, so I'd avoided it. I doubted most people would even remember I'd been a student there. I'd just kind of blended into the walls.

I guessed that was part of the reason I was so pleased when Dylan noticed me. Out of all of the women he could have chosen, he'd chosen me. The one who was too shy to show her face, that wouldn't have said a word to him if he hadn't spoken to me. But he had seen me, he'd spoken to me, and he'd chosen me to be his, even if it was only intended to be for a little while.

I had sometimes felt like an actor in my own life, portraying what others had always wanted, or expected, me to be. With Dylan, all of that had changed. I could be me. I could talk about the things that bored other people, like a tidbit about history that I'd learned, or about the principles of business management with Dylan, and he'd always discuss the matter with me. He wouldn't tune out and let me talk just to appease me; he'd actually hold a conversation with me.

Now, I'd find out if that was all finished and done with, or if we could go back to what we were last week. I realized I'd been standing in front of his door for quite a while when I heard the elevator ding behind me.

I hadn't even heard it go down, but I heard that noise. There was only one person it could be, and when I turned around, I saw him there. There was surprise in his eyes, shock even, but there was also a deep hunger that was oh so familiar. I felt my insides respond instantly, and my skin went tight all over.

I was going to say something, I didn't know what, but Dylan didn't give me the chance. In an instant, I was in his arms, and I felt how cool his skin was against my face when he kissed me. His hands pushed my hips back against the wall, then he tilted me into him as my arms went around his neck.

Dylan kissed me, his tongue entwined with mine, and neither of us cared that we were in a hallway. It wasn't like anyone would come by and see us, so it didn't matter. I clung to him and kissed him with every ounce of passion I had to give. He tasted of scotch and Dylan, a taste that was so familiar, but always made me hungry for more. I inhaled his scent and felt the coolness of his leather on my fingers.

With ecstatic glee my fingers then plunged into his hair to hold his face to mine, because I never wanted this kiss to end. Burning heat flooded my veins, and my movements became slow. His kiss slowed in turn, but it didn't stop. Not at all. He pressed himself into me and hitched me up just a little, until I was on my tiptoes and barely hanging on to him. It didn't matter because Dylan was there, he was in my arms, and he was kissing me. Nothing else mattered.

He broke away for a moment and stared at me, his lips pursed, and I thought he'd say something. Instead, he closed his eyes on the look of anguish I'd caught a glimpse of and pushed me into the wall with another earth-shattering kiss.

I felt lightheaded, giddy with joy, but I didn't pull away. I didn't want to break the spell because I knew I would if I tried to speak, I'd ask him something stupid like how his day had gone, or if he'd got his laundry done today, almost anything but something that could be seen as sultry or seductive. I had that knack for ruining things if I wasn't careful.

I wanted to speak to him, but right now, this seemed far more important, and he wasn't asking for a contract, so I decided to let it go. I'd see how far we got, and then I'd give him an offer. Two weeks without a contract, just to see how it went, and if he didn't like it or couldn't cope, we'd go with a contract.

Or if he wanted a contract, I'd sign it; I didn't care right now. I just wanted him to keep touching me. His hands ran up my jacket, and he hummed happily when he found my skin bare. I pressed into the cold touch of his fingers against my hot skin. Something about the contrast made me want more, and I let him know it.

I was sure it was only the fact that he was touching me that really mattered, but why examine the logic of it at this point? That would just be stupid. I was not a stupid woman. I wrapped myself tighter around him and tried to get closer. I just wanted to be closer to him. I knew about his past now, I knew what had driven him to the life he had, and it made me hurt for him. I wanted to take his hurt away, all of it, and take it into myself where he didn't have to feel it anymore.

I'd never quite felt like that about anyone

before. Not that deeply. It scared me, but it was new, and new things always scared me. I'd decided at the outset that I'd face my fears and work past them. I'd do my best to live for this moment of my life. I knew now I'd fight for every moment I could have with Dylan, but I knew he was fragile in one regard. His history might not allow him to take this any further than friendship and sex. If that was all he could give me, for now, I'd take it.

I'd worry about the rest later. Right now, I'd wanted to make sure I never saw that anguish in his eyes ever again. I didn't want to be the reason it was there either. I'd wash it away somehow. I'd replace it with my care. I'd tell him all of that as soon as he let us both come up for air. Until then, he could have me right here in the hallway if that was what he'd wanted. I didn't care anymore. I'd just wanted him, and that was all that mattered, in the end.

Chapter 6
Emily

"Well, hello there, Dylan," I whispered when he pulled away from my lips and then pulled me up in his arms. My legs wrapped around his waist as he pressed me against the wall. I felt his excitement as a pressure against my center and wanted to grind myself into him even more.

I slid up the wall a little higher as Dylan gave me a smirking grin, my arms still wound around his neck.

"Hello there, Stephanie," he whispered as his lips brushed against mine. "You've been a very bad girl; you know that, don't you?"

A shiver of excitement slid down my spine and made my skin prickle with anticipation. That was all he'd needed to say for me to know I was going to be punished for my willfulness. It was a playful moment, however, not one that made me afraid.

His broad hands held me up, cupped beneath my bottom, as he held me there. "I'm going to make you regret every moment we spent apart."

His cologne filled my nose as his head moved, and his lips started a dance along the length of my neck. When he bit down on one area, I went a little weak.

"I'm sorry, Dylan." It was a pant more than an apology, but I'd said it, at least.

"I know you are. So am I, because now I have to make sure you understand the error of your ways."

As if that was a threat, I thought, but didn't say out loud.

I'd been wet from the moment he pushed

me against the wall. Now, with his tongue against my neck to soothe the place he'd bitten, the tension in my abdomen grew, and the need to feel his skin against mine became almost unbearable.

I turned my face away from his and gasped for air for the reasoning abilities it would take to form words.

"Let me down, Dylan." I didn't think about what he'd said, I just felt, and my body demanded things more than my brain could think.

"No, ma'am." Instead, he carried me through his doorway and into this kitchen. He placed me down on the long, dark table and slowly removed my clothes. I didn't have on much, so it didn't take long before I was naked against the cool top of the table, my feet on the edge. He'd arranged me that way, no words, just actions.

Now, he moved my feet apart. I felt his stare as if it was a touch. His eyes wandered down from my face, down to breasts. My nipples went impossibly tighter, and then the skin over my abdomen. His gaze went lower, to the pink slit between my thighs.

"Mm. Good." He didn't elaborate; he just looked. "Turn around, Stephanie. Let me see the other side of you."

This time his fingers trailed along my shoulders, down my spine, into the crevice of my ass. I gasped when he pulled my hips out and pulled up until I moved with his touch. I realized then he was positioning me. I braced myself against the table, ready for him, more than ready. This entire time I'd wondered if he'd deny me his cock. He did that sometimes, when he felt I'd been bad and needed a reminder of who was in charge.

Sometimes, he'd let me have it with my mouth, but that was it. He wouldn't fuck me, and that was torture. We'd been apart too long, though, and he'd needed me, needed what only I could give him. My hard nipples pressed into the cold plane of the table barely warmed my body, and the contrasting temperatures made them burn. If only he'd suck them, make the burn an ache.

I didn't care if it meant I had to wait for him to fuck me; I needed relief for my nipples. He didn't do that. Instead, he moved behind me and then I was being pushed into the table, my face pressed down, as he thrust into me hard and fast, until he filled me entirely with his cock.

"Oh yes, Dylan, that's it," I gasped, unable to control myself, my nipples forgotten. "Fuck me, baby."

"Shut up, Stephanie," he ground out as he started a punishing pace. His fingers dug into my hips to keep me in place, but I still moved in time with each of his thrusts.

"Fuck you, Dylan." A little bit of anger brought the brat out in me, and I disobeyed. I knew it would get me something extra out of him.

He pushed deeper, his fingers went tighter,

until I felt the bite of his nails on my skin. His grip didn't let up, and the burn of little crescent moon-shaped indentations on my skin made me hiss happily. There it was, that little bit more.

The sensation of his cock moving inside of me stole my breath away suddenly, and I wanted to laugh with happiness. Spread over his table, my ass in the air, I could not have been happier. I was so close to the edge of satisfaction that I knew I'd explode any moment, but I'd held back; I'd wanted to wait. He'd taught me that little trick. Wait for it, don't rush into it.

I tightened my walls around him and got the response I'd wanted. He grunted a sensual guttural sound that made me go tight involuntarily. I gasped out my own surprised pleasure and let my face settle on the cool surface. It soothed the overheated skin on my cheeks and brought me back to the world for just a moment.

I'd wanted to shock him, to let him know I still had some of my control. I slid my hand down to the place where we were joined and grasped him between my fingers.

His reaction was immediate and shocked me. Instead of fucking me even harder, he pulled out, his hand on my ass as he stepped away from me. Then his hand came down against my ass. Hard.

"That is not what good girls do, Stephanie." He did it again, in the same spot, and I knew my skin must have been red. The area burned, it itched, but the other untouched side of my ass was jealous. I squirmed against the table, my fingers splayed as I sought for something to grip.

"Sit still, madam," he instructed, but I couldn't. I'd needed too much; I'd needed everything.

His hand came down on the other side at last, and my head tilted back just slightly with gratification. It burned so good. Hard enough to make my skin red, but not to bruise me. Again, the hand came down, then to the other side.

I felt it edge closer every time, to the sensitive skin lower, and I tilted my hips up to encourage him. I'd wanted it. I'd wanted this punishment, the insane goodness of his slap against my nether lips.

"Please, Dylan. Sir." I licked my dry lips and asked him for what I'd wanted. "Please slap my pussy, sir."

"Oh, is that what you want, brat?" he asked, and I felt him move up behind me, as he lowered his head down closer to mine. His cock dug into the globes of my ass, and I squirmed all over again. "Do you want me to make that pretty pussy cry, pet?"

"Yes, sir. Make it cry, please." I knew I was begging and didn't care. I'd wanted his attention, all of it, however he chose to give it to me.

His fingers moved and touched the smooth, petal soft skin with a delicate caress, but he didn't slap it. He just soothed the wet flesh, but it didn't soothe me a bit.

"Dylan," I breathed his name, my longing for him a fire within me. "Please, sir."

He moved, and I knew he'd knelt when his fingers touched my ass to open me up to him. His lips brushed against my bare vulva, then his tongue delved down to the pink bud that ached the most for his touch.

His tongue came out, flicked at me to lick up the juices my excitement had created. I'd cried out with relief when his lips finally found my clit and closed over it to suck at it roughly. I loved it. My hips bucked up to meet that sucking mouth, before he gave me a long laving lick that made me almost scream.

I could just picture the image we'd created with him behind me, his face between my soft ass cheeks, mouth buried in my pussy while his fingers moved to follow. One dipped into my wet heat to lubricate it before he moved up to the puckered skin he now displayed to the world. He'd played with the area, teased me before, but he'd never actually fucked me there. Would that be part of my punishment tonight? Something lurched in me, and I hummed, vibrated maybe, with excitement.

I tensed as his finger pushed against the skin there, asked for entry. He slowly pushed the finger deeper inside. I'd shuddered beneath him, powerless to stop him, because I didn't want to. I'd wanted to know the world Dylan had to offer me, the world he drove me to explore. I couldn't help the way I'd moaned as his finger slid deeper into me, or the way I'd panted as he invaded my body.

I flexed my hips, wanting to take more of his finger, wanting more of him inside of me. Maybe, if he stood up and slid his cock into my pussy too … oh fuck, I was going to come.

"Sir," I panted, so close; fuck, if he moved out of me, or deeper into me, with his finger and his cock, in both places, I'd die a very happy girl.

Dylan, always the sir, my dominate, the decider in our sex play, pulled his fingers and mouth away and stood. For a moment, he plunged his cock into the soaked walls of my velvety depths, but then he pulled out. I started to protest but he moved so swiftly, without even a hint of gentleness, that I didn't really have time to say anything.

A moment to reposition himself, both hands on my bottom, to hold me open and to also hold me down, and then I felt him there. It was a slow invasion, careful and gentle now, as Dylan *pushed* into me. I couldn't help the shudder that shook me, but it wasn't revulsion. It was an invasion that shook me. It felt ... good.

For a moment there was pain, and my muscles flexed around Dylan.

"Push past it, Stephanie. Make your body let me in." His words were strained, and I was in such torment now. He'd brought me close to orgasm so many times now, only to pull away. I hadn't complained, I'd accepted it, but this was extreme for me, totally new, and I had no idea what he meant. He could tell me to relax all he wanted to, that didn't mean I had a clue as to how to go about it.

My brain wouldn't work, and I had no experience with this. All I could do was breathe. The fat head of his cock inside me held tight by some ring of muscle that didn't want to open. His fingers dug into my hips in frustration.

"Stephanie." It was a warning, one that made me inhale quickly because it was so thrilling. What would he do? Just fuck past the barrier?

"Sir," I started, but didn't know what to say.

"Flex the muscles there, Stephanie. Work them until I'm in." He pushed insistently against me, and I tried to do what he asked.

"Relax, Stephanie," he said as he stroked softly at my back. "Just imagine how full you'll be when I get my fingers in your pussy too, pet.

As soon as you let me get my dick in your ass, I'm going to fill you there too."

That created visions, and I licked at my lips, eager for it. For a moment, the thought of being filled in both places flashed around in my head, and I felt my body relax at last. Dylan sank into me then, deeper, filling me, and the shudder coursed through me all over again.

"Sir."

I wasn't sure whether to move or not, so I let Dylan guide me. He pushed in deeper, but I didn't think there could be more of him. I was so full, opened so wide I didn't think I could take anymore, but I did. I took every inch he could give me. Warm liquid drizzled over my ass, slid down the crack, and the glide of his cock inside of me became much smoother.

I didn't care what it was, it must have been some kind of oil, maybe cooking oil, or salad oil; I knew he had some of that on the table, but it didn't really matter. All that mattered was how full of him I was. I gave myself up to the sensation he created in me as he fucked my ass and concentrated only on what I felt as he moved within me.

I held myself still, this first time a little too overwhelming. Dylan pushed a little deeper, a little faster, until he was making quick, short thrusts inside of me. It felt good, so good, but he didn't do what he'd said he would. He left my pussy empty, he didn't fill it at all, and now it was killing me. I'd wanted to be full, so full, of only him.

Dylan gave me the freedom to fantasize, he'd even talked me through some rather raunchy fantasies quite a few times, but I didn't want anybody else I only wanted him and this world that we'd created together. I didn't need anybody else to touch me, to bring me to the places that he took me to.

I could feel him inside of me and wondered if he'd come in me back there. I'd felt my body clench, and a gasp escaped him. I grinned, a dirty, nasty grin of satisfaction. I'd made him do that. I tensed my muscles again, now that they knew what to do, and worked myself back against him. I reached for the orgasm that was there, but somehow knew he wouldn't let me have it, not yet.

With one last thrust, Dylan exploded inside of me, and my body clenched again, but not with fulfilment. This was jealousy, because I'd wanted that oblivion. I'd wanted that moment. It didn't matter, I knew that this was what I'd wanted for the rest of my life; I'd wanted whatever Dylan decided to give me. Even if that was an exquisite punishment. I'd take it.

Chapter 7
Emily

"What do we do now, Dylan?" I wound my fingers with his and sipped at a small glass of wine.

We'd had a shower, raided his fridge for nibbles, and had settled onto his couch together. I'd wanted to fall asleep after that reunion, but I knew we needed to talk. We couldn't ignore the problem and hope it would fix itself.

"What do you mean?" The words vibrated through his chest as I settled against him once I'd put my glass down.

"I don't want to ruin this moment, Dylan, but we really do need to have a very long talk." I had to smother a yawn, exhaustion really was taking over now. I hadn't slept well since the last time I'd slept with Dylan in the bed. "We need to talk about what we're going to do now."

"What do you want to talk about, pet?" he asked, his hands sliding down my arm to pull me more tightly to his side. I held onto that moment, memorized exactly what it felt like to have my legs thrown over his, wrapped in one of his long, terry cloth robes. I even memorized what it felt like to have his lips against my forehead.

"I want to know how long we're going to do this, how far we're going to go." I tightened my fingers on his smooth chest, afraid of the answer he might give me. Would he ask me for a contract right away, or would he listen to my offer?

"Well, what do you like, Stephanie?" he

asked, his hands tight now on my arm, but not in a punishing way. He was just as nervous as I was then.

"I'd like to propose something." I paused to take a deep, calming breath before I finished. "I want you to give me two weeks without a contract, just to see how you feel about it in the long run. If you want another contract after that, I'll give it to you. Does that sound acceptable?"

"I'm not going to say no. I think I have to admit that this is more than just a fling, don't I? I can't get you out of my head, even though I keep trying." He let my arm go to swipe his hand over his face, as if to clear the cobwebs from his thoughts. "I would prefer to have a contract in place, and we really should have one, but..."

He paused, and I thought that he might be on the verge of taking it back. I could see the indecision in his eyes when I pulled back to look at him.

"Can't we just have a little while without one? Just to see how it would be?" I wanted to know because I knew I could show him that we didn't need it. I would never do to him what his mom did to his father.

That was another problem. Did I tell him I knew, or would he have assumed I'd Googled him once I found out his name? Would he want me to bring it up? Suddenly the mood changed, and I was tense all over again.

"If that will make you happy, then we'll try." His voice held a tension I didn't like, but I felt him relax.

I knew this was all new for him, it was for me too, but we could muddle along together and make it work. I was sure of that.

My body was still on fire for his touch, and as he held me against him, I knew that would not ease. He'd decided that I would not be able to have satisfaction, and contract or not, he meant to be dominate in this relationship. I'd bow to that.

Roxie had said I was a brat, even Dylan had called me that, and I guessed that meant something in their world, but in mine, it meant I wasn't easy to get along with. I'd pout, and whine, and kick my feet over the smallest things. I wasn't like that at all, but with Dylan, I kind of understood the term. I had to be defiant because that was part of the game.

The problem was this had all become far more than just a game. It was a relationship. He hadn't spoken about much of anything, and we'd gone silent again already. I knew we needed to talk about this all, and I needed to tell him who I was, and what I knew about him, but it didn't feel like the right time. Not when he'd only just let me back into his life.

"You know I'm still not a relationship kind of man, don't you, Stephanie?"

I cringed but not because of his question. That was another secret, one I should have already revealed, but he'd hated Trent. I was afraid if he knew I was Trent's sister, then he'd think I was just doing this to fuck him over. At the same time, I knew not telling him was just as incriminating. It would look like I'd been hiding it from him for bad reasons.

I took a deep breath to try to calm myself. I'd have to tell him eventually, especially if this went on for much longer. I wanted it to, and that meant I'd have to tell him.

"I know, Dylan. You've said it often enough." It was my job to be lippy, wasn't it?

"Pardon?" He pulled back and looked at me. "Was that some kind of sass that you just gave me?"

Ah, the game wasn't finished for the night then. I wasn't sure if I could take much more of his punishment tonight, but if Dylan wanted to play, then I wasn't about to turn him down. I turned in his arms, but he lifted me and stood, rather than kiss me as I'd expected. He'd carried me through his apartment and when he passed his bedroom door, I knew where we were headed.

The room he'd constructed, the black room where he could do anything to me, anything he'd wanted to. I tensed, and a shiver of anticipation passed through me.

"Do you consent to the things I will do to you in this room, Stephanie?" he asked as he sat me down. I sank to my knees, my brain already in the sub zone.

"Yes, sir. I consent to the things that you will do to me in this room." If that was all he required for now, I would not argue.

"Give me your hand." He pulled me up and moved me to a new area. When had he done this?

"The workmen came while you were … away. I thought you'd like it. I can strap you down in a variety of ways. First, stand here." He went to a stand that was his toy box. He came back and gave me a set of ear plugs, a mask that would slide over my head, with an opening for my ears, nose, and mouth, and clamps. Those were placed to the side for now.

"Put that mask on, pet," he ordered, and I did as instructed. He opened the zipper that allowed my mouth to be free and then gave me the ear plugs.

I rolled the silicone plugs in my palm, hesitant. I wouldn't be able to hear anything. The world would be silent. I was already blinded by the mask, he wanted to take my hearing too? I took a deep breath, and then, put the ear plugs in.

That's when he guided me to the new construction. A round barrel-shaped area, made of stained oak wood, with clamps, chains, and cuffs in a variety of areas. He pushed gently, and my heart raced. Face down I could at least have some dignity. Right now, he'd taken everything from me, even my independence. I was a little afraid, not of him, but of what might happen.

Wasn't it odd to think being bent over was

at least more dignified than facing your dominant? I pushed the thought away and tried to concentrate on the senses I had left. Touch, taste, and smell. There wasn't anything to taste, so that left me with two senses. I held my hands out, and he then placed a cuff around them. The cuff was connected directly to the clamp, and I couldn't move away.

My heart raced again when he clamped my feet wide apart. That was when my brain went into overdrive. It could be anyone behind me; he could be playing a game and letting someone else touch me. The thought had scared me, but it also exhilarated me. It was dirty, even nasty maybe, but something within me had responded to that.

I wasn't necessarily after degradation, but being used and taking in return? That kind of thrilled me, and I couldn't help it. That was my nature. I didn't want anyone else but Dylan, but, if he told me to, as my sir, then I would probably do as he had instructed.

I felt fingers on my lips and opened my mouth. My head was almost upside down, so it was a bit awkward, but I soon found a way to give his cock the attention he wanted. I knew it was him, I could smell the scent of his skin, and I knew the way his cock felt in my mouth. The buzz of fear quieted, but that didn't make my body stop throbbing.

If anything, his hard cock in my mouth had made it worse. I had desires, needs that had to be met, needs that had already been tortured, but this was more. It was enough to drive me mad. I couldn't see, I couldn't hear, and I felt very isolated.

It was good, I'd liked it, but it was also a prison of its own, this dark silence. His hand came up to hold my head still as he fucked into my mouth over and over again. My lips were going numb from the friction of his cock sliding in and out, but I couldn't complain. My mouth was more than full.

His thrusts came quicker, deeper, and I

knew he was close. He'd let me down after he came, but I should have known better. If Dylan brought me in here, he brought me in to play, not to get off quick and then go to bed. He pulled out of my mouth at the last minute, and the cuffs on my hands were released. He moved around to where my feet were also clamped down and pulled me up.

It was only a moment before his hands guided me back down. This time, I was face up, my breasts and vulva exposed. The barrel was big enough that my head hung halfway down the barrel on one side and my legs hung down the other. More clamps and my hands were restrained over my head, and then my feet. I was stable, I wouldn't fall off, but this new position made me wonder. The other had felt alright, but this position messed with my balance.

I was about to protest when he pushed a ball gag into my mouth and clamped it together behind my head. He was done with my mouth then. My teeth closed gently onto the ball, but they would not meet. Now, I only had touch and smell.

I could smell my own scent by now, the scent of my arousal as he teased me, even if it wasn't direct. Not until the point when he put the nipple sucker on my left nipple. That was when my hips jerked, and my feet pulled against the cuffs around my ankles. The second one went on, and I began to move around on the barrel, not to get away, but because I couldn't sit still.

Locked into my own world now, I was free to go where I'd wanted to, be what I'd wanted to be, as long as it was a woman strapped to a barrel. I'd wondered if he'd fuck me again. Would he be able to since I was tied down to the barrel? I didn't know, but the idea thrilled me. His hands moved down my body, over my stomach, and to the slit that had my most tender pleasure zones.

Another clamp, this one on my throbbing

clit. Let's just say, it didn't help matters. My skin felt like it was on fire, and the blood rushed around my body madly. I couldn't help the moans that came from behind the ball gag, so I didn't try to stop them. I just took what he gave me and knew it was my punishment.

That was made clear when Dylan pulled the sucker on my clit away. I'd been so close, just right there, and I'd screamed in frustration. It was more of a yell of anger, which would not help, but I couldn't stop it. I panted, like a caged animal, afraid and panicked. I was in pain, but it was the exquisitely evil sensation of pleasure that made me hurt. It was a pain that had burned, but I'd wanted more and more. All that he could give me. All that I could take. And then a little more, just to make sure.

I screamed again when his mouth replaced the sucker on my clit. He'd sucked at my pussy, at the smooth lips, and my clit, and then he went down to lick at my entrance. It was even worse than the sucker. Fuck, I was going to die. My heart was just going to explode, and that would be it.

He did something, and the suction on my nipples became tighter. It was excruciatingly good, and I thought I had stopped breathing. I could swear my heart had stopped beating for a second at least, when his mouth went back to its play.

"Dylan!" It didn't come out that way around the ball gag.

I was there … just one more tilt of my hips, just one more breath, and I'd be there. I was desperate for it now. It was so close. Oh, Dylan, please, I'd thought, let me come.

He didn't. He moved, pulled the suckers from my nipples, and removed the cuffs. I stood there, shook to the core, and still burning with need. I'd do whatever he asked of me. I didn't care, as long as he let me come.

He'd guided me to something and pushed

against my neck. We moved together as he arranged me on the leather table. My legs were out in front of me, my back pointed straight with my head pointed at the wall, not the ceiling. I couldn't figure out what he had planned now, not with me in the shape of an L.

My nipples zinged with the sensation of the blood moving around them, and I started to squirm. I got a smack on the ass for that, but then his hand ran down to my pussy. He cupped it for a minute before he grabbed my hips. With one swift shove he was inside of me.

Only this time, I was still locked in my own world. I couldn't hear him tell me not to come, and I couldn't help it; I was a greedy bitch, and when he plunged into me the tenth time, I'd come apart. The friction of my thighs pressed on my clit and the sensation of him fucking me was too much for my overstimulated nerves. I blew apart and this time, it wasn't just my heart that had stopped.

I quit breathing because my lungs seized up

on a scream. I felt every inch of him inside me, and I'd come hard around him. I hadn't cared if I'd squeezed him too hard, or if I'd broke his cock at this point. I'd come and hadn't cared about anything else.

Chapter 8
Dylan

I thought I might have been … happy. Two days later, I was sitting in the dining area of my apartment with the most beautiful woman I'd ever bedded. She was telling me about her day, and her smile was infectious. I couldn't help it, just her presence made me feel calm, but that didn't surprise me; she had always done that to me.

"You told the guy you just wanted your oil changed, right?" It was just a question to keep her talking. She was animated as she told me about how the garage she'd taken her car to tried to give her an entire list of things that were wrong with the car. It was brand new; there wasn't anything wrong with it. They were just trying to pull one over on her.

At least she was smart enough to know that. She'd asked for her keys, paid for the oil change, and had left. She had looked down, saw my glass was empty of wine, and had poured a little more. She'd cooked a dinner for us, and I ate every bite of the homemade four-cheese ravioli she'd made from scratch, along with the sauce she'd prepared.

I'd let the contract thing go for now. She'd asked for two weeks, and I'd agreed to give it to her. It would cause another argument to disagree, and the moment I'd seen her in the doorway, I couldn't say no to her. I couldn't say no to myself; my body hadn't let me. From the moment our lips met all over again, until the point when we finally went to sleep, tangled together, I'd thanked fate for bringing her back to me.

That terrified me, but I'd examined those tender edges of emotions that I'd blocked out long ago. For now, I'd just wanted to be with her again.

It was nice to come home to her, with music in the air, the smell of food ready. It had almost reminded me of when I'd come home from school to find Dad in the kitchen. I'd clamped down on that quickly and went to Stephanie to kiss her and give her a hug. It had felt good, like the world had suddenly dissolved into only us.

I had news, but I didn't want to share it yet. Everything had been agreed on the resort I'd wanted to buy. The current owner had the final papers in his hand, and the real estate agent said the rest wouldn't take long after that. Papers had to be filed somewhere, and deeds had to be applied for. The state would drag its heels, I was certain, they always did, but I'd own the place soon.

I'd given her the single rose I'd bought from

a street vendor, and it rested now in a vase on the table. She'd got this look in her eye when I gave it to her, like she'd wanted to cry but had swallowed it down. Was the flower wrong? I thought women liked roses! She kissed me and thanked me for the flower and now her eyes landed on the flower. She got this far away look, as if she was in a happy place. So I knew it was a good thing then.

I didn't ask her about her family, and she didn't ask me about mine. From that, I gathered that she had her own past history to contend with. She'd never said anything about them or alluded to them in any way. Maybe she didn't have any.

It wasn't beyond reason to think that. In today's world people died in car accidents, from drug overdoses, got caught in the crossfire of gang wars. Hurricanes, floods, and other storms took others. There was always something. Or maybe her parents hadn't wanted her.

My father, at least, had wanted me. Mom had only wanted me to ensnare my dad. After that she'd barely had anything to do with me. They called it post-partum depression at first. She'd leave me crying for hours in my crib, in dirty diapers and wet. Dad had to hire a babysitter to take care of me while he was at work. She'd go out, as if she didn't have a child waiting at home for her.

She'd always been like that, up to the day she'd died. She'd said she loved me that night, but it wasn't a good kind of love. She'd loved that I'd brought her Dad, and she'd been told time and again that she was supposed to love me. She just hadn't been able to. She felt guilty that I'd lived and breathed, and if anything, she'd regretted my existence.

I'd pushed up from the table and tried to rid my brain of the thoughts that plagued me now.

"I have cherry cheesecake for later. Or now if you'd like?" She'd looked up at me, eager to please.

"We can have it later. Shall we go for a walk? I need some air."

"Sure. Let me grab my jacket."

I was glad she'd decided to join me. I held her hand as we went down to the front exit of the building and headed for the boardwalk. It was a bit windy and the air carried the smell of the saltwater. Seagulls screamed overhead, even though it was almost dark now. They were noisy, but amused Stephanie.

"They're so big. I bet they could pick up a small animal and carry it off." She'd moved to my side and put her arm around me as we walked along.

The boardwalk was empty right now, and we'd made it down to an arcade before I knew it. "Care to go in?"

"I've never been in an arcade." Her eyes were wide with excitement. "Let's go in."

She'd put her hand down into the back pocket of her jeans and pulled out $50. The jeans were topped by a burnt amber pullover sweater, and she had on black low-top boots. She was sexy, even in her casual attire.

"Hmm, should we make a bet?" I asked and gave her a smug grin.

"A bet on what?" Her head tilted slightly to the left, and she looked confused. It was so sweet.

"Well, you see, you get tickets for all the games you put tokens into. The one to come out with the most tickets, wins."

"What do we do with the tickets?"

"You usually turn them in for prizes. Care to take the bet?"

"Of course. You're on, buddy." She had no idea what she was betting on, but she didn't care because it was me she'd made the bet with. She knew she'd like whatever I chose as my prize.

Just like she'd loved the other night when I'd tied her down to a wooden barrel and teased her into perdition. Then, I'd let her have what she'd wanted the most, and it had been beautiful. Whatever I came up with as a prize would be equally beautiful.

An idea occurred to me, and either way, I knew we would both win. We went into the arcade and bought some tokens. We started off on the easy games, the games for the kids like Whack-a-mole, and moved up to video arcade games and a few others. We raced in simulations on racing motorcycles, and to my surprise she'd beat me on that one.

We turned our tickets in, and Stephanie used our tickets to get a giant penguin the arcade had behind on the shelves, then we left, happy and laughing.

"So what's your prize then, sir?" she asked with a gleam in her eye. The lights had come on overhead, and her eyes glistened in the light.

"Have you ever been to New Orleans? I have a few days free and thought, well, it might be nice to wake up with strong Cajun coffee and some beignets for breakfast."

She didn't answer right away, and I'd

wondered if I'd said something wrong. "Sure, yeah, that sounds good."

That didn't answer my question, though. "Have you ever been?"

"Yeah. Uh, a few times. I never really left the hotel I was at, though, and it wasn't a big deal. Not like this sounds like."

My old Stephanie was back in an instant, and I'd pulled her close. It didn't sound like she'd had any fun on that trip to New Orleans. I'd make sure she had a lot of fun on the next trip.

"Is tomorrow too soon, pet?" I asked as we walked along, arms around each other.

"No, not at all. I don't have anything planned. I'll just need to head home this evening to pack some clothes."

"I'll drive you over."

"Oh, sure, thanks."

I really didn't want to spend a moment without her that I didn't have to. Which was another thing I wouldn't examine right now.

Once we'd made it back to my apartment, I set up a private charter to take us down to the Big Easy, booked a bed and breakfast in the French Quarter, and arranged for a car to pick us up at the airport. After that I'd driven her to her place, and she'd made sure she had everything she might need.

I'd noticed that Stephanie never asked for money, and her home was filled with name brands and very expensive furniture. Whoever she was, when she wasn't with me, it was someone with money. I knew when I met her at the bar that she came from money, though. The way she spoke and the way she held herself all screamed of private school.

The luggage she'd rolled out of her bedroom was also a luxury brand. It wasn't a big deal; it just meant one thing was certain— she wasn't after my money. In fact, it didn't surprise me a bit to find out the money I'd given to her as part of our arrangement had all gone to local charities.

No, that would never have to be a concern.

Not that I had any, not really. She didn't want to sign a contract, well that was her business. Other than that, Stephanie was sweet, beautiful, intelligent, and fun to be with. She had an infectious laugh that invited everyone around her to join in the fun. Her smile lit her beautiful face up and made her even prettier.

She was generous, kind, and, dare I say it, loving. I'd learned what that meant from my father and my adoptive parents. Otherwise, I wouldn't have known. The world had been a giant asshole to me.

After my adoptive parents took me in, they'd sent me to therapy and to a local private school. The kids there had been merciless to the white trash kid taken in by the rich people who had been duped into feeling sorry for him. For a long time, it had hurt me, but over time, and with the love of my new family, I'd got past most of it.

I'd come to expect little from the world but hurt, and I had arranged my life around that. This celebratory trip to New Orleans might be misguided, but either way, I'd get to spend some time with the woman in my life in a beautiful setting. It could be magical in New Orleans, and later that night, after she'd gone to bed, I'd made a phone call.

"Hello, Celia," I said into the phone when a woman's sultry voice came over the line.

"Oh, Dylan, you devil. It's been a long time." The older woman, ageless but with a mature voice that gave her age away, spoke into the phone with a purr.

"It has been, and I'm coming down tomorrow. Do you have anything going on at Pepper's?"

"We do, indeed. What did you have in mind?"

"I have a, uh, friend." I heard a soft chuckle of amusement. Celia knew I didn't do relationships; she must be dying of curiosity with that little admission. "She's a bit on the innocent side, but she wants to explore what the world has to offer. I thought of you and your place."

Peppers was a secret sex club, exclusive to those in certain income brackets. People like me. It catered to requests, when made, and sometimes held special events.

"I think I can arrange something. Is she one of your usual types?" Celia purred down the line.

"Not at all. Something totally different. She wants to explore things like voyeurism, exhibitionism, and BDSM. The usual for your club usual, really."

"I think I can put together something for tomorrow night, babe. Around nine pm good for you?"

"Sounds perfect. Thanks, Celia." I smiled as I turned the phone off and headed to bed with Stephanie.

She was a warm, soft lump beneath the

covers, and I'd pulled her body close to mine. I didn't care if I woke her up or not. I was selfish for a moment, because I'd needed her to reassure me that I wasn't insane. I'd exposed myself to so much since I'd met her. I'd relived memories that were better left buried and had questioned my own sanity. I still did, but she made me not care whether I was sane or not.

She made me not care if we were in a relationship or not, despite my protests. All that mattered was that she was there, and I didn't have to ask her for anything. She gave me all I'd needed plus some.

Chapter 9
Emily

I'd always wanted to go to New Orleans, I'd thought as the plane touched down and we'd prepared to exit. Rather, I should say, I'd always wanted to go as something more than my brothers' secretary or babysitter. I'd never had the chance to explore the place or to look around. I was always doing some task or taking care of the kids. I'd rarely left the grounds of our hotel in the city. The times I left it was to find a pharmacy for something the kids had needed, and I'd taken a cab.

I'd never been able to experience it properly, so to me this was my first visit. It was a place of fantasy for me, a place that movies and books promised was magic. I could now find out just how magical it really was. I'd read about it in dozens of books, looked up places online to visit, but there'd never been a chance to stroll the streets and explore.

Once, Jesse brought me back some cold beignets, and a couple of times I'd ordered the sweet confections through room service, along with a nice cup of café au lait for breakfast, but I'd never gone out and had a po' boy sandwich, or anything like that. I'd never visited the graveyards that were famous the world over, or seen the countless sites that had made the city famous for hundreds of reasons.

This was a chance to get to do as much as a person could do in New Orleans in a short amount of time. I'd looked over at Dylan with excitement in my eyes and grinned. It wasn't even nine am yet. The time went back an hour here, and that gave us extra time.

"What are we going to do first?" I was like a kid let loose in the candy store, and I was all but bouncing with my excitement.

He'd booked us a bed and breakfast, something else I'd always wanted to try, and had found the perfect one. It was full of antiques and very private. As we were the only guests, it was also going to be very quiet.

"We'll get checked in and drop our bags off. Then, we'll explore as much as you want to. We have plans later this evening, so don't exhaust yourself too much with the sites today. We have two days, and we can always come back later. I'll have to get back to Myrtle Beach for some business, but we can come back once all of that is sorted."

We got into the back seat of the black car that waited for us, and the driver pulled out of the airport. Before I knew it we were speeding along the highway.

"I'd love to come back when we have more time. Thank you, Dylan." I'd smiled and leaned into his arm as the city passed around me.

The car sped down an exit, and before I knew it we were pulling up to a gated two-story home. It was everything I'd dreamed a bed and breakfast would be. The exterior was done in that style that screamed Louisiana, right down to the iron scrollwork on the upstairs balcony. The house was painted in a faded gold tone, but it was a pleasing tone, and the whole thing just screamed romance. To me, at least.

I couldn't stop smiling and the woman who greeted us, the owner I'd soon found out, gave us a tour of the home before she showed us our room. My heart melted, and I couldn't dim the grin that spread over my face. There was the antique four-poster bed I'd dreamed of, right down to the mosquito netting to keep us safe from the evil creatures as we'd sleep. A large window to the left side, just down from the bed, let in the morning light.

"It's perfect, thank you." I'd turned to the owner, and she'd smiled.

"I'm glad you like it. I'll be in the living room if you need me." She left us then, and I did what I'd been aching to do since she'd opened the door.

I walked up to the bed and then jumped onto the mattress. "Oh, God, it's so soft!"

It was like being on a cloud, and even Dylan's chuckle of amusement couldn't dim my happiness. He came to the bed and climbed up over me.

"Happy then, pet?" He'd kissed the right side of my face softly and pressed his hips into mine.

"Very happy, Dylan." I'd put my arms around his neck and kissed him with gratitude that soon turned to something more stirring.

"No. Not right now," he said and pulled back, a smile in place of the passion that had just been there. "We have streets to explore. Come on, get those incredibly sexy but impractical heels off, and put on something you can walk around in."

I didn't want to leave the bed, but I did want to see the place. I groaned, but got up to dig around in my luggage for some flat shoes. I'd found a pair of white canvas shoes and put those on. At least I'd had some sense and put those in my bag.

We were soon in the hustle and bustle of the French Quarter, and I could smell and see so much that had already started to endear the place to me. I didn't know why it hadn't occurred to me to come down here after I'd left the role of secretary and babysitter for my brothers. I'd gone to Myrtle Beach because it was a familiar refuge.

I should have come down here, I'd thought, but then, I wouldn't have met Dylan. I'd snuggled in close to his side, and we'd stopped at a café to have a light breakfast. The smell of coffee, cinnamon, and vanilla wafted from the entrance, but we'd decided to sit outside. It was cool, but not too cold, so we'd stayed outside at a table there to enjoy the sunshine.

"There's a shop here in the French Market that sells quaint little local art. We'll head down there after we eat, if you'd like." Dylan sipped at his coffee and took a bite of his breakfast sandwich.

"That sounds good to me. I want to see it all." We'd already passed a lot of bars and jazz bars that were closed at this hour, but would soon come to life as the hours passed. We'd stopped at a couple of shops and passed more than a few colorful people already.

I couldn't wait to see what the night brought to life. I'd savored my first taste of the square donuts covered in powdered sugar from a proper cafe, but we were soon walking again. Before long we were in a shop filled with more things than I could imagine. Soaps, dolls, paintings, statues, and hand-blown glass filled every space.

Dylan picked out quite a lot and arranged to

have it shipped to him in Myrtle Beach. I bought a few paintings and some of the glass art for the house, and that was being delivered to our bed and breakfast. I'd take it back with me on the plane when we went home.

We headed back to the bed and breakfast soon after that and had a nap. It was nice to snuggle down with Dylan, and I'd wanted to do more than cuddle, but he told me to behave, so we slept. After that we showered and headed out to eat.

The streets were lit by ironwork streetlamps and the bright lights from shops and bars. I'd smiled as we walked to a gourmet restaurant owned by a Cajun chef. We'd ordered gourmet versions of Cajun food, and it was delicious, but I'd wanted to know more about this 'date' he had planned for us.

"What all did you bring with you, clothes, I mean?" he asked as he wiped his mouth and pushed his plate away.

He was dressed in a casual black suit, and I

had on a burgundy wrap dress with long sleeves. I had a black one that matched it with me, and a white dress, with a full pleated skirt and a box neckline. I didn't think either would be suitable for a night-time event.

"I don't think I have anything suitable to wear."

"That's fine, I know a place. Let me just arrange for a cab." Dylan went and talked to the maître de and soon came back.

"It's all arranged. Are you done?" He'd looked impatient, like he was also a bit on edge. Where was he taking me?

I'd soon found myself in a rather romantic looking boutique, looking at a variety of dresses. I had no idea where we were headed, but I figured I should be looking for something sexy. Dylan had disappeared then quickly came back with a dress that I would never have picked out.

"Try this on." He'd said it in that tone, the

one that had said he was aroused and wanted me to play the game.

I lowered my eyes and let a hint of a smile play around my lips. "Yes, sir."

I took it back to a changing booth and slipped the dress on. It was a wrap dress too, but this one was black material with silver sequins covering every inch. Cut in an asymmetrical style that left my left thigh bare as well as most of my chest, it was sexy. I could imagine Dylan would have a hard time keeping his fingers off the little bow that kept the panels together.

It wasn't something I'd have picked out, but if he wanted me to wear it…

"What do you think?" I leaned in the doorway of the booth, the door open to let him see.

He stared at my full breasts for a moment and then his eyes traveled down. "Oh yes. That one."

I grinned and shut the door. We left the

store and went back to change in our room. I put on the pair of black patent leather heels that he liked so much, with the silk ribbons that wound up to my knees, and slid the dress on. A quick curl of my hair with the curling iron, a little makeup, with a fresh spritz of his favorite perfume, and I was ready to go.

"You look gorgeous," he said and kissed my ear.

"Thank you, so do you." I straightened his tie and brushed his hair back from his face, and we were ready to go.

I caught our image in the reflection of the hired car that came to pick us up and smiled. I was light to his darkness, and it was a good reflection.

"Oh, I bought you this too." Dylan took out something from the bag he'd brought along, and I saw it was a new mask.

This one was similar to mine, but it had less beads and more feathers around the edges. That hard frame fit snuggly against my nose, and I'd turned so that he could tie the ribbons at the back of my head. I already felt like a beautiful woman, but now, sensuality had been poured into the mix. I knew for sure we were headed to somewhere sexy now. If the dress wasn't enough to give that away, this was.

I'd waited, breath held, as the car drove out of the city and to a place on the outskirts. A plantation home?

"Where are we?" I asked and stared up at the line of oak trees we'd passed.

"A friend of mine has a … ahem, home here. She has rather exclusive parties out here in the peace and quiet. For grown-ups."

"I see." A house party? How sexy could that be? I'd been to dozens, maybe hundreds of those. They were never sexy.

The moment we stepped out of the car, I knew I was wrong. This wasn't the kind of house party I'd expected. Music blared from the walls, sensual and erotic, and the sounds of voices filled the air from open windows. I knew why the windows were open, despite the chill in the air, when we walked into the house.

It was downright steamy hot inside. Small gas lamps lit the place, but not too much. There was only enough light to see by, to keep the intimate nature of the party in place. Every room held people in a variety of situations, and I could see more than one sex act taking place. Was that a woman? Oh my, she was straddled over one man, while her mouth was filled by another. I'd looked away, only to find a woman with light coffee-colored skin coming toward us.

She was gorgeous, from her light brown cat eyes, to the body she'd displayed in a long, sheer robe. She wore a barely-there bra and panties beneath. Her black hair was fluffed out and wild, but it suited her.

"Hey, Dylan. Glad you came down to see us." She was taller than Dylan, but that was because of the platform heels she had on.

She'd leaned down to kiss his cheek and then looked over to me.

My cheeks turned red as she looked at me, and I glanced down to the floor, my hands twisted together.

"And who is this?" Her voice all but purred as she'd spoke to me.

"This, Celia, is Stephanie. Stephanie, say hello to Celia."

"Hello, miss." It seemed the right touch, for the moment.

"Oh, she does have pretty manners. Welcome to my home, little Miss Stephanie. I hope you enjoy your time. Here, put this on her. It will let people know they can look, but not touch, unless you allow it."

I glanced up and saw a velvet collar with black silk ribbon for a lead. Now that was a nice touch, I'd thought as I swallowed and tilted my head up so that Dylan could put the collar on me. A leash wasn't something we'd used before, but it excited me. This said I was his, and that really changed things around in my brain.

I was already his sub, but now, on the leash, I felt like that was real. Even if the collar was made of velvet.

"The party has already gone wild in the living room, as you can see. Come back here in the kitchen; it's quieter."

She'd led us through the house and down the length of one side of the three-story sprawling home. She could have made a hotel out of the place, with just the rooms we'd passed so far. We passed opened doors and closed doors, and doors that were slightly ajar, as the occupants were waiting to be joined by someone.

I wanted to explore each one, but Dylan tugged on the leash every time I started to slow. I would resent that, but I knew we had time. We came into the kitchen, lit only by strategically placed candles, and I was happy to see that the room wasn't empty.

In fact, there was more than one man gathered around a young woman sprawled on the table. They were apparently eating their dessert from the woman's body. Different confections decorated her body, and the men were licking and nibbling away at each place. Even her breasts were covered in hardened dark chocolate.

"Stephanie can sit there," Celia instructed and pointed at a chair away from the table, but close enough to watch what went on.

Dylan took me to the chair, and I sat, my attention taken by the woman on the table now. Her eyes latched onto mine, and I could see the arousal in the brown depths. Her body arced occasionally, as a mouth finally broke the chocolate and encased her nipple, or the man who was eating ice cream from her lower abdomen chased drips of ice cream down between her thighs.

The woman bit her lip, but her eyes didn't leave mine. I felt drawn into that dark gaze and couldn't look away, even when I'd tried. It wasn't that I wanted to touch her necessarily, but that I'd wanted to be her, and I'd wanted to experience whatever sensation it was that made her eyes so very … intense.

I'd wondered if she knew the men, or if she'd been hired to let them have their way with her. Or maybe she was a guest and volunteered. It looked like a very messy, but certainly attentive way to get off. The man had finished the ice cream and moved down between her thighs to clean her up more thoroughly. She held her hand out to me then, and I didn't know what, but something made me take it.

Dylan was talking with Celia about something, I had no idea what, because I was too engrossed in the woman's eyes. I watched the wonder, the pleasure, as she'd experienced it, and when her hand gripped mine more tightly, I felt something in me respond. I'd watched as she'd moved suddenly, her body convulsed, and knew that this was her peak. She'd looked incredible, beautiful and feminine, as she gave a loud groan. The men around her, all still dressed, continued to eat from her, or suck sticky, sweet sauces from her skin until she sank down against the table, replete.

Her fingers hung loosely in mine now, and her eyes closed. I didn't want it to be over, though, and squeezed her fingers. She'd opened her lovely brown eyes, decorated with blue smoky eye makeup, and smiled at me. She gave my fingers a squeeze and let go so that she could get up. She'd left the table, and I'd watched her go, disappointed that it was over.

"Don't worry, pet, there's more to see. And experience." Dylan had caught my attention, and I'd looked up at him.

Experience? What did that mean?

"Take her to the ballroom, Dylan. I think she'll like that."

"Ready?" he asked me as he pulled on my

leash, and I stood, ready to obey. And find out where he was leading us to, of course.

I'd walked behind him until he found a blue door. I couldn't hear a lot of noise coming from the room and thought perhaps it was empty. It wasn't.

We walked into a very large room where soft, sensual music was playing. I wasn't sure what I'd expected, but a room full of strangers, dressed up in pre-Civil War fashions wasn't it. Men and women danced, and I'd found it all quite lovely, but not sexy. That was, until I'd noticed the women's dresses didn't have tops that covered their breasts, and that some had their skirts up around their hips as the men with them explored their bodies.

One couple in particular caught my eye, and Dylan led us to a set of chairs close to the couple. The man had the woman up against the wall, his hands beneath her skirt, and the sight excited me.

"Would you like to dance, pet?" Dylan asked, and I'd turned to him, my eyes glazed.

"Yes," I said, and followed him onto the dance floor. I didn't know the steps they were following, but the crowd opened to let us into the middle. We soon caught on, but I'd noticed after a while that dancers were getting closer.

Dylan's hand tightened on my leash, but he didn't stop my dancing. When a woman bumped into me, I'd apologized, but then another one did. The music started to make my head spin, and then Dylan started to dance in some pattern that twirled us around and around. My head swam, and when he'd stopped, it took me a moment to catch my breath.

More hands brushed against me, and bodies came closer. The music changed, became more modern, sensual, and the dancers changed to match the music. Bodies came closer, and I felt hands brush against me once more. Dylan's head came down, and he kissed me as we continued to dance, a more sensual dance that didn't require a lot of moving around.

He'd pressed into me, and I could feel how hard he was for me. I'd looked up at him as a pair of hands came up from behind me to cup my breasts. I'd jumped but stood still, my eyes locked on his. His eyes smiled into mine with knowing, and I let the hands explore me. They fell away, but another pair soon joined them.

We stood still now, and Dylan watched as hands came at me from all directions, but left me open to his view. He sat in the chair and watched as unknown lips touched my neck, whispered compliments in my ears, and hands touched me. My hips, breasts, ass, even my face, everywhere except the one place I wanted to be touched now. The one place only he could touch me.

I had all but forgotten how to breathe by the time Dylan took my hand and led me from the room. He'd stopped at a door with a window painted on the panel, and opened it up. The room was empty, but I could see that it was one of those rooms. The kind where people could look in, only this one would let us see those in the other room too.

"There are people in the room next door," he said as he put a sign that hung from the doorknob on to let others know the room was occupied. "Let's see who."

It was a rather beautiful couple, both in their late twenties, dark haired, and dark eyed. The woman was on her knees, but she'd looked up as we came into our room. The man looked me over, looked at Dylan, and then took himself in hand. He'd said something to the woman, and she'd moved. I couldn't hear what he'd said, but it didn't need explaining.

She'd filled her mouth with him and forgot about us. I'd stepped closer, and Dylan moved up behind me. His mouth came down on my neck as that familiar ache started to burn in my lower abdomen. I'd watched the woman and the man as Dylan's hands came up to cup my breasts.

"He wants you," Dylan said into my ear. His fingers slid beneath the panels of my dress to tease at my bare nipples. I hadn't worn a bra with the dress, and I had no panties on at all.

"How do you know that?" I asked, doubtful. The man was looking at me, but he wasn't doing anything that I would take as a sign.

"He can't take his eyes off of you, pet." Dylan cupped my breasts and held them up, as if to offer them to the man. The man, handsome and Hispanic, with long hair, and a tall muscular frame, lifted an eyebrow.

There was a question there. It went unanswered for now. His hand came down on the woman's head, and she had his attention for a moment. She slowed down, took her time, and I'd watched him now, fascinated. This man wanted me?

Dylan moved my long blonde hair from one side of my head to the other so that he could kiss that side of my neck. "Are you ready for what comes next, pet?"

"What comes next?" I asked, not sure at all.

"I'm going to strip you down and let him see you."

I'd gasped, surprised, shocked even, but somehow, also excited. It felt good to be wanted, and I couldn't lie. I was aroused by the idea of the handsome, dark-eyed man next door watching me. Wanting me.

My nipples were tight, hard, and I'd pushed them against the glass to ease the ache there. Dylan squeezed them hard, really hard, as if to remind me that I was his. I'd groaned and leaned back into him again.

"Do you want him to see you?" he asked close to my ear.

"I, Dylan … I don't know." I wasn't sure how to answer him. A sub would say no, wouldn't they? "I'm only for you. I'm yours."

"So you are, pet." His fingers moved, pulled

at the edges of my dress, and I'd held my breath.

The man next door pulled the woman up from the floor and pulled back from the edge of the bed where he sat. His room was exactly the same as ours. A bed, one table with condoms, and bottles of lubricant and sanitizer, with a couple bottles of water on top. There was nothing else in the rooms.

The woman in the other room, with long black hair and one really hot body, slid up in front of him, facing us. She'd smiled at me and then looked at Dylan. She'd licked her lips then, and I'd felt a pulse of excitement. What would it be like, to watch him … well, with her?

Would he do it? I'd wondered. Would he allow that man to touch me? I'd wanted that man to touch me. I'd wanted him down on his knees, in front of me, his mouth buried in me. "Dylan?"

"Yes, pet?" He'd sounded amused, but he didn't move.

"I want so much, but, I'm afraid."

"I know, pet. We won't go any further than this tonight, so don't worry. Just relax and know that the man in that room wants to fuck you as badly as I do."

"It's so dirty."

"It is, but that's what makes it so very good, pet." His fingers pulled at the bow that held the dress together then, and he'd pulled at the shoulders so the dress would slip away.

I stood there, totally bare, in front of complete strangers. I was glad the rooms were only dimly lit; that made it romantic, at least. It wasn't like a bright light, that wouldn't hide any flaw. This was soft, hidden, and made it okay to be naked in front of strangers.

The couple watched us now, as Dylan's hands explored me. He'd twisted my nipples until I'd cried out his name and sagged against him. Then his fingers went down to tease at my clit. The man next door mimicked Dylan's movements, and I'd watched them.

The woman's head fell back, and she'd closed her eyes. I could see dark nipples on large breasts, her flat stomach, and thick thighs. She was lovely, really, perfect the way she was, and when her hips began to move in time with the man's strokes on her clit, she was even more perfect.

I felt my own move, they matched her rhythm, and somehow we'd all synced up.

"He wants to fuck you both, I think," Dylan said, and I groaned. "I'd let him, if you asked me to."

"I, no, I couldn't." That would just be too weird. It was great as a fantasy, but I'd wanted to leave it there. "Would you fuck her?"

I wasn't jealous, just curious. I didn't own him, and yeah, I'd wanted a real relationship with him, but the idea of watching that really excited me, rather than angered me.

"If you wanted me to," he finally said after a moment to think. "I only want you, though, Stephanie."

Pride flushed through me, and I'd hated to say it, since I was supposed to be exploring my sexuality, but I was more than a little satisfied with his answer. I didn't want to own him, but I had a claim on him, and he'd just admitted that.

"Make me come?" I asked, and he'd gone quiet.

He'd pushed me against the wall to the right of the glass, so that I could see the couple now only from the side. They'd moved, and the woman climbed up on the bed, the man on his knees behind her. Dylan sank down to his knees and pushed my legs slightly apart.

"Open, Stephanie," he demanded, and I'd obeyed.

"Fuck," I ground out when his mouth went directly over my excited clit and began to suck, hard, at the organ. "That's it, Dylan. Fuck, that's it."

I'd wanted him to suck harder, harder, whatever it took, to make me come. I had closed my eyes, but I'd forced them open, to look. I'd wanted to see. The man was waiting for me to open my eyes, and when our eyes locked together, he plunged into the woman.

He had this fierce look on his face, as if he'd wanted to come right through that glass and fuck me, but he couldn't, so he'd fuck the hell out of the woman beneath him instead. For a moment, a rather bitchy moment, I'd wondered if he'd rather be fucking me instead of her. If he'd throw her off the bed and come fuck me if I crooked my finger at him.

I'd cupped my breasts and held my breasts out to him. He'd licked his lips, and my nipples tingled. I'd flicked at them, and he'd grinned. My hips began to move in time to Dylan's tongue, and the man next door moved faster. He'd fucked her harder, deeper, and I'd squeezed my nipples tighter.

Dylan's hands came up to cup my ass, to pull it apart so that he could tease me back there. I blew apart then, hard and without warning. Dylan grunted, but he managed to hang on as I'd forced my eyes open again. I'd wanted to watch the man as I came. And he put on one hell of a show. I knew he was coming, deep inside of the woman in the bed with him. He was staring right into my eyes as he did it. Fuck, it was hot, it was so fucking hot.

I came all over again, all over Dylan's face, and he'd just held on for the ride.

Chapter 10
Dylan

I took Stephanie back to the bed and breakfast after that. She'd come so hard, over and over again, that she'd been too tired for anything more. We'd had an early flight, a lot of walking, and she'd worn herself out. Well, the man next door and I had finished her off, actually.

She'd wanted to crawl up on the bed and go to sleep, but I wouldn't let her. I'd pulled her into a reception area that Celia had in the front of the house and asked the staff member there to call a car for us.

"Dylan, you didn't…" she started to say but didn't finish.

"It's okay, babe. Tomorrow." I didn't even realize I'd called her that until she looked at me funny. "What?"

"Nothing, you've just never called me babe, before." She'd curled up against my side on the bench we were on and hummed happily.

The couple from the room next door came out, both fully dressed, and the man gave me a smile. I'd nodded back, in control all over again. I wasn't sure I'd ever let either one anywhere near Stephanie, but it had all been fun to fantasize about with her.

They'd asked for a car of their own, and then the man came to me. "Pardon me. I don't mean to be rude, but if you two are interested, we'd love to take you out to dinner sometime."

I'd looked at the card he'd held out and took it from him. Stephanie sat up beside me, but she'd clutched at my waist.

"We're only here for a couple of days but

may be back soon. We might just give you a call." I took his card and put it in my pocket. I'd talk to her about it later, when she'd let the idea sink in a little bit more; after I'd decided whether I could let another man actually touch her without killing the guy.

It was nice to be polite in Celia's, though, and the man hadn't been rude, so I'd stayed cool. It was up to Stephanie anyway. Everything was when it came to that kind of thing. She was new to all of this, and I didn't want to scare her away from anything. I'd wanted to let her find her own boundaries, not force her to submit to ones I'd imposed on her.

Which was kind of odd, I'd thought as the man walked away to sit on the other side of the room with his partner. I'd wanted a sub, a woman to make my own, and Stephanie had offered me an opportunity to mold a woman into exactly what I'd wanted. She'd been a virgin, completely new to all of this, and instead of bending her to my will, I was letting her bend me.

She'd started to open my own mind about what life was about, and maybe that wasn't a good thing, but it was happening. I didn't want to fall in love and have a family, but a relationship didn't seem as disgusting as it used to. I'd already spent far more time with her than I ever had any sex partner before, and now, here I was, taking a card from a very polite stranger who had offered dinner. I knew that offer came with a lot more behind it than a night of food.

He'd been suave about it, at least. I could appreciate the balls it took to walk up to me.

I didn't think we'd ever make it to that point, only if Stephanie would want it. Well, we'd cross that bridge if we came to it. I'd looked over at her, and she'd gave me this cheeky grin that I had to turn away from. I would have laughed out loud if I hadn't. She looked so cute, so self-satisfied, that it had made me want to break out with laughter.

I'd looked back, and the grin had grown. "Fuck, you're an evil little minx. Stop that."

I'd said it quietly, near her ear, and she'd just winked at me. The little minx winked at me!

"You said he wanted me. You were right."

"So I was."

The conversation was interrupted by the driver of the car coming in to lead us out to the car. Stephanie's mask was still in place, but I took her leash off and gave it to the person at the reception desk. We'd left and didn't look back, although, I had a feeling Stephanie had wanted to.

I wouldn't have minded staying longer, but my woman needed some sleep, so sleep she would get. We'd got back to the bed and breakfast around 1 am, and I'd used the key given to us by the owner to slip in quietly. Stephanie took a shower and slid into a cute little flannel nightgown. By the time I came out of the shower she was asleep.

I'd tucked in behind her and pulled her to me. She didn't wake up, but she did push her ass into me, which caused a small problem. Ha! Make that a big problem, I'd thought as my dick grew hard as a rock. I'd decided to wake her up in the morning and get some relief. Then, I'd take her down to Jackson Square and somewhere else. Somewhere not sexy, I'd decided, as I'd tried to get my erection to go down.

To the graveyards, and maybe to the church. Perhaps we'd go to a fortune teller or somewhere, but then I fell asleep and didn't finish the thought.

* * *

I woke up with the smell of her hair in my nose, but her head wasn't anywhere near my nose. Somehow, she'd slid down in the bed and her mouth was now over my dick. God it was so wet, so hot.

"Mm, Stephanie. Don't stop." My words were lazy but pleased. I'd let my fingers tangle in her silky hair as she'd sucked at my cock, just the way I'd taught her. She'd become rather good at it, almost too good. "Slow down, I want to enjoy it a little longer."

She did as I'd instructed and I'd patted her head. I'd felt her fingers grasp at me as she'd pulled her lips away from me. "Good morning, sir."

"Good morning, pet. Now go back to sucking my dick."

I heard a soft chuckle, and then my eager little sub went down on me all over again.

I'd let my hand reach out until I found her ass, and I'd slid my hand down between her thighs. She was rather pale, but I'd liked her that way. My hand slid down her silky thigh and found dampness well before I'd reached her center. She was soaking wet and ready for my fingers.

"What were you dreaming about that got you so hot, Stephanie?" Which was a stupid thing to do because she had to let my dick go to answer me.

"That man last night, and his woman. They were hot." She went right back after her quick, unembellished answer.

Mm, my little sex fiend had a sex dream, did she? I'd wanted to know more about it, so I'd pulled her off of my dick and pulled her around to straddle me, with her face right above mine. "Tell me."

"I, mmm, wait." She'd stopped talking as she'd sank down onto me and shifted around to find just the right spot. When she'd found it, she sighed and started to rock on me. "I was with all of you, in this big ole bed."

I had to agree, this was a big bed. I looked around the room, decorated in white and noted for the first time just how much white there was. White walls, white furniture in the form of a wicker chair and a painted white cabinet. Even the end tables were white, as was the small desk in one corner. Everything was white. I took notice of all this because I was trying to distract myself.

Stephanie's tight, wet pussy straight after her mouth, was always too much to take. I'd have come right away if I didn't distract myself. Maybe it had been stupid to ask her about her dream, because now that her mouth was free she'd elaborated on it.

"I was taking turns with you. He'd fuck me, and then you would, and then you'd fuck her, and then he'd fuck me, and it was just this sort of, well, train, I guess. I don't know, but it was all night long, and when I woke up, I had to taste you. I had to have you, so I thought that would be the best way to wake you up."

"Mm, yes, so it was." I pulled her down and sucked at a nipple until it was hard and stiff, then did the same to the other one. I felt her walls clench around me, and let my right hand fall down to where her slick body joined mine. I found her clit swiftly, and started a pace that would have her in space in no time.

I watched her, and that made it hard to stay in control all over again. She gave herself up completely when she fucked; there was no part of herself that she held back, and it made the whole thing even more erotic. Watching women get off had always been a thing for me. Some men like to watch women's asses move, or their breasts; they liked to watch other men getting off on women, for some reason I'd never quite understood, but for me, it had been watching women get off.

Stephanie did it beautifully. The way her face softened, every squint of her eyes, and the way she parted her lips was a work of art that burned into my brain. Watching a woman come was amazing, but Stephanie made it more than that. She made it an experience that you couldn't resist.

Even now, just watching her expressions as she moved on me, and fuck, she moved just, was something to watch. She pushed herself up as she grew closer to that final moment, and I watched her breasts dance for a moment. Now that was beautiful, I wouldn't deny that. I glanced down to watch her slim waist move and saw the place where we were joined. That was something else, incredible, but her face always drew my eyes. Even when I could watch myself slide into her, I'd still rather watch her face.

She gave a gasp, the right kind of gasp, the kind that said I wouldn't have to hold on for much longer, and I pressed into her clit just a little harder. Just enough to make it more enjoyable for her, to change it just enough, and she arched her back on me. Mmm, I thought, as her tight nipples pushed into the air, now that was a beautiful picture.

I pulled her down to me, to watch her face as she came apart on top of me. I couldn't hold back anymore, not when her open mouth hissed out a breath of a scream. She was trying to hold back because we were in the bed and breakfast. Still, her face said it all, and when she squeezed around me one last time, I let myself go.

I held her to me, tight, so close, and let myself empty into her. I breathed in her smell, and it took me to a brand new place, one that only she could take me to.

She slumped down on me, and I held her in my arms. We shivered together for a moment, and then we were both still. It was done now, but we both knew the passion, the need for each other, was never far away. I kissed her softly on the back of her head and just held her.

This was something else that I'd only ever done with her. Only she had ever made it feel good. Like it was the right thing to do. Her legs were still straddled over me, but her torso clung to mine, her arms were around my neck, and I knew this closeness was something else she craved. I knew that because I did too.

"God, you feel so good, Stephanie." I turned her over and looked down into those fascinating gray eyes of her. They held so many secrets, but so much delight.

"You feel good, too, Dylan." She smiled a happy smile. "I need to go to the bathroom. Let me up."

We both laughed, and she got up to put on a robe. The sun was just breaking into day, and it was early. Good. We had all day to traipse around New Orleans then. We ate breakfast with the owner. Hot buttermilk biscuits with sausage gravy, bacon, and eggs, all made by the owner. Served with a cup of coffee and a glass of orange juice, it was the perfect breakfast to keep us going on another day of walking.

She gave us some advice on places to visit, and it wasn't long before we were out all over again. Around an hour later we stopped on a park bench and sat under a huge old oak tree. We watched people going back and forth, and a man came by selling balloons. I got him to come over and bought two pink balloons from him and gave them to Stephanie.

"What are these for?" she asked with a laugh.

"I don't know, I just wanted to buy you something silly." I pushed her hair back from her face and looked into her eyes. "I'm really glad we came down here."

"I am too. It's been so incredible." She looked out at the scene around us and smiled. People walked all over the place, cars drove by, and voices from all over the country could be heard. Some even sounded like maybe they weren't from America. People from all over the world came here.

I'd been here before, but I'd always been alone. It was a totally different place when you were with someone who mattered. I backed away from that thought because I didn't want to examine how much Stephanie meant to me. Not right now.

"Come on, let's go look at that shop with the weird dolls. Those things looked scary."

"Oh my God, if you want to, but yeah, those things are scary." She stood with me, and we left the bench, headed toward the other street. I really wanted to get her away from the jewelry store, because as I'd sat there, I'd started to notice the engagement rings and wedding bands in the window. What was worse was, I'd wanted to go in and buy Stephanie a ring. That was scarier than any doll had ever thought about being.

Chapter 11
Emily

I thought this man of mine might need therapy. Probably a thought that many women had before I ever came along. Countless women throughout generations had probably had the same idea that their man needed help that they couldn't give them.

Mine wasn't bad. He wasn't mean, or evil, he didn't brutalize me, and leave me doubting myself. He didn't dominate me and make me feel like property, but he did leave me feeling hurt when he talked about contracts. He'd brought it up again the night before. We had four days left before I either had to agree to a contract or face heartache all over again.

Life had become good since we'd come back from New Orleans. Something had really changed down there. Dylan mostly, I thought. He was sweeter, the way he made love to me was softer, and even when he took me to his special room; he was gentler and focused only on my pleasure.

He was a softer man, to me at least, and it was melting my heart. When he came home from a day out, or even if he'd only gone for some shopping, he'd always bring me something back with him. A box of chocolates from a shop he'd found, or a trinket of some kind. He'd brought me a dress from an antique shop he'd come across one day, a rather breathtaking black velvet dress that was a timeless masterpiece. I didn't know when I'd wear it, but I'd wear it for him if an occasion didn't come along.

He'd suddenly turned into a boyfriend, and that made me nervous. He'd mentioned the contracts again last night. I'd pretended to be asleep, but I'd heard what he'd said.

"I'll take you back to New Orleans in a couple of weeks. We'll have a contract then, and maybe we'll have to amend it a little. If you've thought about that couples' offer."

When I didn't answer, he turned his light off and curled around me. I couldn't avoid it for long, though, and I knew it. We were both in trouble now. I knew why he'd wanted a contract now. Or I thought I did. I'd been willing to sign a new one, when I came to him, but he'd accepted my offer.

Now, I just wanted to avoid the whole conversation. I knew why he'd wanted it, that didn't mean I liked it. I didn't like it at all. The problem was, I seemed to be the only one who didn't understand why it wasn't a big deal.

Even Roxie had started to get a bit ticked off with me about it. "Just sign the damn thing and be done, Emily."

That was what she'd said later that day, when we'd met for lunch.

"Get over your fears and sign the contract. You're his sub, you do get that, right?"

"That's it though, I don't think I am. Not anymore. I think I'm something different. Oh, I'll get down on my knees and do what he asks when it comes to sex, but outside of that, there isn't much domination going on."

"Really?" She was curious, I couldn't fault her for that. Dylan was an anomaly. A dominant who had veered into a boyfriend. The fact that we'd met at the club made our relationship odd too. Then there was the fact that he still had no clue who I was.

"Really." Not that I was complaining about it, I was just being honest. "He doesn't seem to be anything like I had imagined he would be."

Oh, he could still be dominant during sex,

and he was always an Alpha, but that didn't mean he wasn't also caring, kind, and even gentle at times. I sighed heavily and looked away. I saw Jesse, my sister-in-law, heading into a restaurant across from the one we were at, and tensed up.

"What's wrong?" Roxie looked around, ready to beat down whoever had upset me.

"Nothing, just my sister-in-law. I was worried Trent would be with her."

"No change on that front either, then, huh?" She looked at me with sympathy, but I brushed it aside with a smile.

"No, it's probably for the best. There's no way I'd give up Dylan now." Although, I did wonder if Jesse had seen me and pretended she hadn't, or if she really hadn't seen me at all. She used to be my best friend.

Another deep sigh and I finished my tea. "Let's go get our nails done, my lovely friend. I can't sit here anymore."

We'd finished our lunch and had agreed to

go together to get the chore over with. I chose a pale pink with glitter that looked as if it was suspended in glass over top, after the gel was set and polished up with a topcoat. Roxie chose an emerald green and much longer nails.

"What are you doing with your free time now, Em?" she asked as we walked to a coffee shop for one final chat.

"I'm writing a book. A children's story, actually." It was something I'd started when we came back from New Orleans, and I'd watched a small boy playing with a puppy. The boy had reminded me of my nephews and had made me miss them. I'd found that writing a story for them helped ease the pain of not seeing them.

"Oh that sounds fun!" She looked at me with excitement. I thought she'd been teasing me, but she wasn't.

"It's interesting. I have a whole series planned, and I'm trying to decide whether to make it for small children or for bigger children reading longer stories, without pictures. If I'm going to make it for young children, it will need pictures, and I'll have to find an artist." I carried on for a little while longer, and Roxie encouraged me to keep the project up.

Which was another reason I really loved that woman. She'd always encouraged me to reach for my happiness, and she'd helped me get that in more ways than one. I'd thought about that as I finally drove away and headed to Dylan's place. She'd told me to just sign the contract. I knew I should, but something irked me about it.

It was more than my bratty nature. There was something about the idea of signing the contract that made me feel like we were taking a step backward. We'd moved past that point in our relationship; I thought I'd shown him that in the last few days. If he was already talking about it, and we had four days left, then he had every intention of bringing it up again.

Did he want to take a step back? I'd imagined Mr. No-Relationships probably did, but I wasn't prepared to do that. I cared about him, I cared about him deeply, and I wanted this to go further. Maybe not marriage, kids, and a home in the Hamptons kind of further, not right now, but definitely a let's only fuck each other and agree that we sleep together at night without a contract, kind of further.

I didn't need Dylan to tell me he loved me and declare his undying devotion, but no more talks about contracts would be nice. Just a normal relationship. Even if that wasn't what I'd said I'd wanted all those weeks ago.

Dylan had shown me far more than the fact that my body loved sex; he'd shown me that I'd had an emptiness in my life. An emptiness that I suspected only he could fill. I drove to his place with urgency, making me impatient. My body did love sex with the man after all.

"Hi, babe. Do you want to go out for dinner, or shall we cook?" he asked as I stepped into the apartment. He'd just come out of the shower. Mmm.

Wet, hot skin, just out of the shower was one of my favorite things. "I think, mmm, yes. Right there."

I backed him up against the wall and slid down to my knees. I caught a sparkle from my new nails and grinned as I opened the robe. Those things were going to be distracting, but not as distracting as that.

I took his already hard cock in my hand and took him as far as I could take him, until he throbbed in my mouth. I loved those pulses that signaled his blood was pumping through him hard and fast. Dylan just let me do as I pleased and dug his hands into my hair to steady himself.

"That's so good, Stephanie." That was something else. He'd stopped calling me pet as often as he used to. Oh, he would say my name, but he rarely did when we were having sex.

I liked it when he called me pet, but when he growled my name, even my fake name, it was so much sexier. I could die happy, if the last thing I ever heard was him saying my name like that. Even if it wasn't my real name.

That was something else that ate away at me. He still didn't know who I was. It was a huge omission on my part, and one I knew I was bound to pay for sooner or later. I was the forgotten Thompson, though, and I could hope that he'd forgive me, once he found out.

I didn't slow my attentions, but for a moment longer, I was distracted. How could I say I wanted a real relationship with him, if he didn't even know my name? I looked up and saw his eyes were on my face as I worked on him. I winked at him, and he had my whole attention once more.

With a practiced technique, one that he'd taught me, I got him close to the edge and backed off. He groaned in frustration, but he didn't protest. He just waited on me to finish my slow tease of his dick with my hand and patiently took what I offered.

"You're going to kill me one day." He gasped when I finally took him in my mouth again.

"I hope not," I whispered before I went down on him, all the way. This time, he took over and started to fuck my throat as I did the best I could to breathe around him.

There was a moment when I wondered if this was wrong, if maybe I shouldn't use sex as a tool to avoid that talk, but I dismissed it. It didn't matter, not right now.

I swallowed around him, and that finally did it. He went over the edge. I took everything he had to give me, and when he was done, I stood up with a happy grin. "Hi, honey, I'm home."

I kissed him, went into the kitchen, got a glass of wine, and looked in the freezer. "Do you want to order something, Dylan? There's not a lot in here."

I turned to see him standing in the kitchen, against the wall. The panels of his bathrobe were back together now, and he had a satisfied look on his face. "I liked that."

"What?" I asked, my head tilted to the side a little.

"That hi honey part. That was … nice." He seemed embarrassed and looked away. "It's not something I've ever heard real people say."

"Not even your adoptive parents?" I held my breath. I hadn't meant to say it out loud.

He looked uncomfortable for a minute, but then he relaxed. "No, not even them. Only you."

"Well, then, that makes it special." I walked up and pressed myself to him, then gave him a wine-flavored kiss. "What shall we eat? I'm starving."

"What do you want?" His hands were on my waist, and I couldn't help but feel like this was one of those moments when I showed him what our life could be like without a contract.

"I'd like whatever you want, Dylan. I'm not picky for once."

"Well, if we order Italian, I have time to take

you to bed before it gets here. If not, I won't have time for anything but maybe a nice warmup to the night's events."

"Oh my, that is a choice." I made my eyes go wide and then grinned. "But if we eat first, and I have a shower, then we can call the night done, and just go to bed."

"That sounds like the winning plan." A strange look came over his face for a minute, but it passed.

I saw it, a look I'd seen before, but he always carried on, as if nothing happened, so I assumed it was some pain he didn't want to talk about. It seemed to be happening more frequently, though, and that concerned me now.

"Are you alright, Dylan?" I asked as he went to get his phone.

"I'm fine, just a twinge in my back. No big deal. Do you want the lasagna meal for two or something different?"

"That sounds fine." I let the question go and headed for his shower.

I didn't like the fact that he was in pain, but if he could keep it under control, then I shouldn't worry too much, I guessed. I went to the shower, cleaned myself up, and came out with wet hair and no makeup. The poor man knew what I looked like with a naked face, and that was something people rarely got to see from me.

I'd been putting on makeup, expertly, since I was thirteen years old, and my mom had sent me to an expert to show me how to apply it. I'd updated the look as the years changed, but it wasn't so different really. Oddly enough, Dylan preferred me without it anyway. Which wasn't to say he didn't like when I had it on, because he did. It just wasn't important to him that I keep it on.

I went into the living room, and he turned on the television. There was a new show we wanted to watch, and when our food finally arrived, he went down to get it, so I didn't have to get dressed. The elevator would open onto a parking garage, so it wasn't like anyone would see him except the delivery driver.

After that, we ate, and once the show had gone off, Dylan led me into his play room. I grinned, because I knew it was going to be a long night, if he was taking me in there. A night where no contracts would be mentioned, because he would be too busy driving me to orgasm, only to pull me away until I would come uncontrollably. It was always a good night with him, no matter what we did. Tonight wouldn't be any different.

Chapter 12

Dylan

I stared at myself in the mirror the next morning. After a swipe to remove steam from my shower, I saw my own reflection and grimaced. I was smiling. Damn it.

I reached for a towel to smear more of the steam from the mirror and found I was still smiling. I looked closer and saw my gray eyes were happy too. Even when a twinge of pain made me grimace, my eyes were still happy. What the fuck was wrong with me?

It was Stephanie that was what it was. Even without a contract, the woman just made me happy, and that was just, well … it was kind of gross. At least to the man I was before I'd met her. He would have hated that look on my face, and he'd have run far, far away.

I didn't want to run away from her now, which was a big problem. It was one I was trying to come to terms with. It was brand new to me, this need to have someone there when I came home, but not just anyone. I also found I slept a lot better when she was by my side at night. When I could wrap myself around her, protect her, I could sleep.

That I could understand. The need to protect was something I knew well. I could deal with that. This *need,* though? That was freaking me out.

"You've got to snap out of this, Dylan. You aren't that kind of man. She deserves better than you. She deserves someone who can love her properly." That finally brought a stony glare to my face that hid the sadness those words actually made me feel.

I had some business to deal with today, a meeting at the bank to make sure the money could be transferred once the current owner of the resort finally cleared everything and got the papers back to my lawyer, and I'd be gone most of the day. I didn't even want to leave her for a few hours; that was how bad this was.

I knew when I had to walk away from that jewelry store in New Orleans that I was in some serious trouble. I'd force some time apart if we hadn't done that already. I'd have snapped if she hadn't come to me. I'd have gone to her, and I knew now I didn't want to give her up again. How could I deal with this?

The contract. That would keep a wall between us. A business transaction, I had to get it back to that, and then, perhaps, my head would clear. I kept that thought in my head as I finished my shave, got dressed, and left Stephanie in bed asleep. There was a note on the bedside table, and I'd give her a call later.

As I drove out to the bank, I found my

thoughts kept drifting back to her. I wondered if she had a passport. If she'd loved New Orleans, she'd really love Paris. Which made me wonder if she spoke any other languages. I'd have to ask her tonight.

I'd learned a very simple version of Spanish and had spent some time learning Dutch. I'd even spent a summer in Amsterdam after I graduated from high school. I hadn't used the Dutch in years, but the Spanish had been useful. I didn't mind it, and I felt that the practice of using a different language helped to keep the brain healthy.

I bet she'd learned French in high school. Most of the girls I'd met back then had taken it instead of other languages. I wasn't quite sure what was so romantic about it, but then I got strange looks when I said Dutch was a beautiful language. I tapped my fingers against the steering wheel and eased the car into moving as the light changed to green, distracted by the need to pay attention to the road now.

Of course, once I got to the bank, the person I was supposed to be meeting with hadn't arrived yet. I took out a notepad I kept in my briefcase and started to write out a new contract. This one talked less about payments and duties, and more about what I'd like to see happen.

My needs had changed as I'd come to know Stephanie a little better. I no longer wanted a pure sub, a woman who was totally submissive to me in all things. I wanted that fire that Stephanie had found in her time with me. She'd gone from a scared little mouse to a confidant young woman who demanded her due. I loved that about her and was more than a little proud that I'd brought that out in her.

That didn't mean I would stop our games or empty out the play room. It just meant I couldn't give her that kind of relationship where I beat her. I'd never had that kind of relationship with her anyway, but she'd wanted it at the beginning.

I checked my watch, saw the manager was a half hour late now, and continued to write. It wasn't necessarily a contract, but a letter. It was a proposal of sorts. Live with me, be my mistress, and I will reward you for that. Hmm, perhaps that wasn't an offer I should make.

Maybe I should have just done what I knew she wanted and let the whole thing go? No, I decided as the manager finally walked in, an apology already falling from his lips. I was a businessman. It was what I was good at. Love wasn't my area. I'd work on the contract tonight. There had to be one. I needed that wall up between us, and I needed it up now.

I'd be in a whole lot of trouble otherwise.

I'd decided to take her out by the time I got home. There was a great little place that played some of the more sensual songs from the 1960s on certain nights and all the people would come out, young and old, to do some of the classic dances from that time. I didn't exactly know them, but it had been obvious that both Stephanie and I knew a few dance steps. We could figure it out.

"Do you have a dress you can dance in?" I asked with a gleam in my eye as I walked into the penthouse, and she came to hug me.

"Of course, I do. What kind of woman do you take me for?" She grinned.

"The kind who deserves everything she's ever wanted. What's that I smell?" I planted a kiss on her nose and followed my own into the kitchen. I found a pot of chicken and dumplings on the stove. Very yummy. Stephanie was also a very good cook.

A woman with many talents, she never failed to impress me.

"Where are we going?" she asked as we finished dinner, and she put the dishes in the sink.

"Well, why don't you go fancy yourself up,

babe, and I'll wash these dishes up? Then, I'll show you where we're going." I smiled as she grunted and stomped off. I'd seen that pleased smile on her face before she left.

A half hour later she came out of the bathroom with her hair pinned up in something I thought was called a French twist, and her face was made up. She wore a pink dress with a frilly skirt and a plunging neckline. Sheer fabric covered her arms, down to her wrists where satin formed the wristband. It was sexy but oddly virginal. Just like my Stephanie.

The dress wasn't so over the top that she wouldn't fit in, but she'd definitely catch an eye or two. Couples came dressed in suits and ties, with formal dresses, while others came in jeans and sweaters. It was just one of those places where you could spend the night dressed however you wanted to.

She was nearly bouncing with curiosity by the time I pulled into the parking lot. I heard the strains of Lloyd Price's version of *Stagger Lee* pumping from the place. The shagging was in full swing then. We walked in, and I heard a gasp from Stephanie.

"What are they doing?" she asked, her eyes glued to the dancers on the floor.

"Well, that, my dear, is called shagging around these parts." The dancers twisted, swung, and grooved along the floor, in a style totally unique to each dancer. "It's kind of based on the old swing dance styles, but the people around here gave it their own twist."

"Wow, look at the couple." She pointed at two people who were really getting into it, and I smiled.

"Yeah, it can get pretty, um…dirty." I looked down and could almost see the lightbulb going off in her head.

"Oh! Kind of like *Dirty Dancing*, the movie?"

"Kind of. I think there's a movie from the 1980s about it, maybe it was called the same thing; I can't remember now." I found us an empty table, and we sat.

"I just can't, wow! I can't understand how they can do that. It's so quick!" She was obviously enamored with the dancing, and I ordered us both a glass of beer from the waitress who came to our table.

"I want to know how to do that. It's amazing!" She turned to me, and I could see she was serious.

"I thought you were from the area?" It was a little confusing, but then, sometimes, Stephanie was. It almost seemed like she'd lived in a bubble.

Then I remembered all the signs that said she'd lived a very sheltered, but rich life. Her manners, the way she carried herself, the fact that she knew how to dance modern dance moves, but also ball room dances. I knew she came from a rich family, one that was very privileged. And perhaps she'd escaped from that.

"I've lived quite a few places, actually. Myrtle Beach has just always been my favorite." I remembered how she'd once said she wanted to go to Iceland. She'd mentioned some of the places she'd been to, but she suddenly seemed saddened when she spoke about them.

"Do you speak any other languages?"

"Huh?" she asked with a surprised smile. "Well, I speak a smattering of Mandarin Chinese, some Italian, Spanish, and German."

"Whoa. All of that? You didn't have time for French?" I thought that was funny, but I knew she wouldn't understand why.

"No, it never really interested me. I was too busy studying the other ones and never really liked it. Oh, a song we can dance to!"

"Shall we?" I asked and held my hand out. She took it with a grin, and we went out on the floor.

"What is this song?" she asked when I pulled her into my arms after a rather dramatic twirl.

"*She's Like the Wind*," I said against her ear

as I pulled her close. "Patrick Swayze sang it in *Dirty Dancing*."

"Oh yeah! I remember now! I can't believe I forgot about that song." She swayed, our steps in time, perfectly matched, as if we'd practiced for the dance.

I brought her back into my arms, placed a kiss on her neck, and thought that Stephanie embodied that song. Maybe I was stupid to think that I could take this further, and she deserved so much better than me. I had a feeling I'd lose my mind too, if she left me again.

"You are magic, do you know that?" A slow smile spread over her face, and her arms wound around my neck.

"So are you, Dylan. You're a fool if you think you don't have anything I need. You have it all, right here." That admission came with her hand softly over my heart.

For a moment, the rest of the dancers disappeared, and I brought her up in my arms to kiss her as I twirled us on the dance floor. There was only us and a kiss that I didn't want to end. The loud cheers of the other dancers and whistles caught my attention finally, and I let her down on the floor.

I was embarrassed that I'd brought us so much attention, but at the same time, proud. Stephanie deserved that kind of admiration and attention. She was every inch a woman, and I had to find a way to hang on to her. Even if I'd be trying to build a wall between us in the next half hour.

It was starting to tire me, this constant battle with myself. Stephanie was mine, and I could have her forever. In the back of my mind was my mother and the way she'd sneer if I ever asked her to do anything with me.

I'd ruined her life. She'd ruined her life by having me, she'd tell me. Wasn't that enough? I'd go away, whether it was a toddle when I was a small child, or I'd walk away with a broken heart, but eventually I stopped asking for her attention. I'd stopped asking for anyone's attention, outside of business.

Even my adoptive parents found it hard to get me to take part in activities with them for a long time. I called them now, and went back to see them, but I never asked for their attention for myself. I thought it still sometimes bothered them, and I knew Mom worried, but I was a grown man now.

Well, I was until Stephanie came along and turned me into a puddle of mud. She'd taken all of my will it seemed, and now, when I was at my weakest, was the wrong time to make decisions.

I'd work more on the contract tomorrow and have it ready for the following day. Then, I'd give it to her. She'd either sign it or she wouldn't. I wasn't sure what I'd do if she refused to sign it or tried to avoid it. I didn't want to end what we had, but I needed that solid wall between us again.

I already had a feeling it was too late to

build a wall around my heart. I'd wanted that piece of paper in place so that neither of us would fall in love, so that we would know where we stood with each other. I had to get that back in place or else we'd both fall. If it wasn't already too late.

As couples gave us compliments when we left the dance floor, and I saw her beaming face, I had a feeling it was far too late. The horse was already out of the barn, as my dad would have said. Both of them.

Chapter 13
Emily

Dylan was still asleep when I got up the next morning, and I let him sleep. I'd noticed last night he'd started to look tired well before his normal bedtime. I knew he had a lot on his plate right now, though I didn't dare ask for details. He'd gone to sleep almost as soon as we got home, and now, he was still asleep.

I hoped he wasn't coming down with something. I went into the kitchen to find something for breakfast and found some orange juice, a couple of frozen waffles for myself, and fried up some sausage while the coffee did its thing. I glanced through the paper that always appeared at the front door every morning.

Nothing new there, the same old misery, doom, and gloom. I rifled through it until I found the comics and the daily crossword and sat to eat and fill in the puzzle.

By the time I finished, Dylan was stirring around in the bedroom. I heard him cry out in pain and ran into the bedroom to check on him. "What's wrong, Dylan?"

"It's just my back. I guess last night's dancing aggravated it. Can you get me an ice pack? There's some in the freezer." He had been trying to get out of bed, I could see that, so I pushed his legs back up onto the mattress and went to fetch the ice pack. I soon had it wrapped in a towel and pushed it behind him.

I put some extra pillows behind him and looked down at him with concern. "Do you need a doctor?"

His back had really been giving him trouble lately, and it was starting to worry me.

"No." He shook his head and spoke again. "There isn't a lot they can do for it. It'll ease off in a little while. Don't worry. Is that coffee done by any chance?"

"Just a second. Do you want something to eat?" I paused at the doorway.

"Not just now, no. Just some coffee would be good." His smile was tight but grateful.

My poor man, in there hurting. "Do you have any pain pills, Dylan?"

"Yes, in the bathroom. I'll get them in a few minutes. As soon as this eases a little."

I poured coffee in to a mug, added some of the hazelnut liquid creamer he liked, and took it to the bedroom. Once he'd taken the cup, I went into the bathroom and looked in the medicine cabinet. I found the pills he needed and brought him one.

"Should you take this on an empty stomach?" I asked as I held the pill out.

He just shook his head and swallowed the pill down with a drink of his coffee. I couldn't do that, take pills with hot drinks, but he didn't seem to choke at all.

"No, probably not, but I need it. This isn't easing off."

"I'm going to make you a hot pack to put on there. Maybe that would be better." I went in and wrapped a dish towel into a pad, soaked it with water, put it in a plastic zipper bag, then heated it up in the microwave. I wrapped that in another towel and took it in to him. "Maybe we should alternate."

He looked miserable, and my heart broke for him. He didn't deserve this, not when things were going good. He'd seemed so happy lately, much less broody and stony than he used to be. He didn't say much about what was going on with the resort, but I knew it must be good. He never came home angry or resigned, like he'd used to.

His phone rang just as I took the ice pack to

the freezer, and I carried it in to him. I knew he'd want to answer it, whoever it was.

"Hey, John. I can't make that meeting today. Tomorrow maybe? Yeah? Good, thank you. I really appreciate it."

I wandered off, determined not to listen. I didn't want any ammunition to be aimed at me when, and if, he finally found out who I was. I'd managed to distract him for the last couple of days, and he'd managed to keep the word 'contract' out of his mouth with great care. He hadn't said it, and there was only three days left.

I thought about the words of one of my favorite songs. If I could go back to the night I'd met him, I'd tell him my real name. I wouldn't admit who my family was because it was a common enough name, but I would tell him my real name. I'd started to hate 'Stephanie'. Even if Stephanie was me. That wasn't my name. My name was Emily, and the secret had started to burn like a destructive fire within me.

I had to get past this contract thing, then, somehow, I had to tell him who I was. Right after, if I was to salvage any of this. Until then, I'd keep my real identity a secret. If we made it past the point of no return, then I'd tell him.

Guilt ate at me, and I poured my attention into making some lunch for him. He'd fallen asleep after the phone call. Around eleven he woke up and tried to get up to go to the bathroom. I had to help him get out of bed, but once he was on his feet, he seemed okay, even if he was bent over a little.

I knew he wouldn't want further help, so I didn't argue with him. He came back to bed, and I kissed him as he settled onto the pile of pillows.

"Thank you, babe," he whispered with a smile. "I'm sorry I'm so useless today."

"No, don't be! You need help, and I'd be a troll not to help you."

"Thanks." He squeezed my hand, and before I knew it, he was asleep again.

Now, I had a light soup simmering for him, for when he woke up. He needed to eat something, or those pills would make him sick. They were prescription pain killers, not just a little dose of aspirin.

Whatever it was, it was something his doctor knew about. I'd seen a row of boxes in that medicine cabinet. I didn't recognize most of the medicines, but I saw one was for neuropathy and another for muscle spasms. Maybe that would do him better, I thought, and got up to get one of those for him.

I put it on the tray I arranged for him once he'd woken up again. He started to binge watch a new show on Netflix by then, and I didn't want to interrupt him, but he paused the show.

"I can't believe this is how I'm spending my day, but I'm damn glad you're here to help."

"I'm glad I can be of help to you, sir." I gave

him a wink and smirk, and he cringed with a smile of his own.

"Oh, don't get me started. I can barely stand up right now."

"I can't help it if having you helpless in bed is sexy."

"Oh, here comes the dom streak! Are you going to tie me down and use me then, Miss?"

I felt my eyebrow lift and my lips twitched as I tried to hold back my amusement. He'd given me such a naughty schoolboy look!

"I will spank you, you know, sir?" I held my hand up as if in warning, and he rolled his eyes and shuddered.

"Oh no, please, miss! I'll be a good boy." He even had the nerve to put on an English accent. The bastard!

I laughed out loud and pecked him on the forehead. "You're too feeble to spank right now anyway. Eat your soup and be a good boy."

"Yes, ma'am," he grumbled, and I kind of liked this pouty side of him.

As he'd said, I did feel a little dominant right now, and I was surprised to find I liked it. The role reversal wasn't something I'd want to continue, but for now, it was fun.

I left him to eat, and when I went back a half hour later, I found his bowl empty, the show had moved on to the next episode, and he was fast asleep. The pain pill must be really strong. Of course, the muscle relaxer would probably make him sleepy too.

I ordered some groceries with a delivery service then made roasted garlic chicken and pasta alfredo, from scratch, with some sautéed asparagus to go with it for dinner. He was fed, at least, I thought, but he was soon asleep again.

He hadn't had more medicine, and that made me wonder if this was more than just a backache. Although, pain could make you sleep.

I thought about those other pills in the medicine cabinet and looked them up. One was for tremors; the other was for inflammation. Well, obviously, he had something going on. I just wasn't sure what. He'd tell me if he wanted me to know, I decided. Or if it was something that would be a problem for me. Meaning, if it was something that I could catch, he'd have told me a long time ago.

It was his business, I concluded. Even if I didn't like the secret. I had my own, though, so who was I to raise hell about one? No, it was better to leave it alone and just take care of him. It seemed he'd already been to a doctor about it, so there wasn't anything more I could do. Unless he became worse.

I spent the rest of the evening in bed with him, watching a few movies I'd wanted to see. He slept through most of it, but he woke up once to go to the bathroom and again to ask for something to drink.

I changed his packs from hot to cold and kept him as comfortable as I could.

Sometime in the middle of the night, he

woke me up. He was wrapped around me, and I didn't think he'd quite realized that I wasn't asleep. Or maybe he was still asleep, I didn't know, but I held still.

"I'm nothing without you, Stephanie," he said when I first woke up. His head was right behind mine, his arms tight around me. "Please, stay with me."

It was a weak moment for him, and I didn't want to say anything. I knew he thought I was asleep, otherwise he'd never admit to something like that. It made my heart race, though, and my skin went hot all over.

Maybe this could work out. One day, we might be past all of this. We'd have no more contracts, no more secrets, and we'd be at peace. Maybe, one day, we'd even have a family of our own, one that we both planned and wanted.

I'd go off my birth control, and we'd just make babies and raise our kids. I was kind of shocked I'd even considered it. I'd spent most of my adult life taking care of my brothers and then their children. I'd thought I hadn't wanted a child of my own, but with Dylan snuggled up behind me, well, I kind of liked the idea.

I wasn't really interested in marriage, but if I could spend the rest of my life with him? Well, that would be nice too. I felt him relax behind me, and before long, he'd started to snore again.

Through the night, he got up a few times, and by the time morning came, he was almost back to himself. I woke up and found him in the living room, the television on and coffee ready in the pot.

"Hi, babe. Thank you for taking care of me yesterday," he said as soon as I walked in. "I bet you're beat!"

"I'm alright. How are you?" I snuggled into his side, and he pulled me in close. It was incredible how much this felt like home. Here, against him, was my home now.

"What are you plans for the day?" he asked, and I leaned back to look at him.

"I have a function to go to around lunch for the charity, and I need to go and check my mail, see if the house has been ransacked. I need to pick up a few things there too."

"Okay. Well, I'm going to be around here if you need me. My back is better, but I'm not sure I can manage a lot of walking around today. You okay by yourself?" He kissed my forehead, and I grinned.

"Of course, I am. I always am. I'll probably be gone most of the day, so if you need to have a meeting here, don't worry that I'll interrupt."

"Alright. Keep your phone charged. I might need you."

"I will, don't you worry." I kissed him on the cheek, got up, and went to have a shower. I was glad he was feeling better, but at the same time, couldn't help but wonder if he was really better. I knew Dylan enough to know the man had a will made of iron, and he was likely just pushing himself to get up.

He wouldn't let someone wait on him for long, I knew that much. That was probably a good thing, I decided as I dressed a little while later. Whatever was wrong with him, he wouldn't complain about it for long.

I dried my hair, dressed, did my face, and left to head to my home first. I needed some papers from there and gathered my mail. I'd go through that later this evening, before I went up to see Dylan. I couldn't take the mail in because he'd see my real name, and down in the parking garage, I could throw away what I didn't need to keep so he wouldn't see it.

By the time I made it to the charity event, a luncheon for local women getting back on their feet, I was focused on what I needed to do. I'd donated a large sum of money to the group and wanted to see how things were working out. Some of the women had needed money for new work clothes and clothes to go to an interview, others needed a grant for babysitting, and others had used some of the money to take classes. Each one was flourishing, but I spotted one off to herself.

I hadn't dressed too swanky, a pair of slacks and a soft white sweater seemed like a comfortable and neutral choice.

"Why are you off to yourself over here, Melissa?" I asked the woman with curly dark hair. Around my age, she had been homeless six months ago, but now, she had a home, a job, and a direction to head in.

"I knew you'd be busy with the others, I didn't want to intrude." She was also very shy, this pretty young woman.

"Melissa! Don't be silly. Tell me how you are!" I smiled at her and pulled her down to a table for a chat.

"I'm good, Emily. Really good. I can't thank you enough. Really." Her smile was as bright as the morning sun, and I felt pride in making sure that smile beamed once again.

"I'm glad to have helped, Melissa. Now come on, stop being so shy, and make some friends."

I pulled her into the group of other women, and before long, she was smiling and laughing, just like the rest. This was why I hadn't totally let my responsibilities go. People depended on me and needed me. I could lose myself in Dylan, but I would always have one foot on the ground for this. It was vital, and I knew I could never let them down.

Chapter 14

Dylan

Symptoms that was all it was. I reminded myself of that as my lawyer left the apartment. The deal was almost done, and I'd had to sign a few other papers for the business, so he'd come to pay me a visit. I shut the door, my hand gripped at the spot that ached on my back. It felt as if the muscle was hard spasm and wouldn't loosen.

I'd gritted my teeth to get out of bed early that morning and make some coffee, but I'd managed it. The doctor I'd seen a few months ago had said things would probably get bad, but I hadn't known it would hurt like this. The good news was, if I kept on the medication and exercised, then I could hold it off. Most of the time.

I went to the couch and sank down; a sigh of relief escaped my lips as I did so. It hurt so much less when I sat. I'd enjoyed Stephanie's brand of nursing and thought how nice it would be if I needed her to care for me again in the future. Not that I'd wish that on her, but if I needed it, I knew she'd be there. She'd still be here today if I hadn't pretended to be perfectly fine.

A new twinge of pain reminded me that love was pain, and pain came with love. Which made me cringe, poetry? That was where I was now? Poetic thoughts?

I found a show on Netflix and turned it on, but time after time, my thoughts turned to the incredible woman I now called mine. I'd really liked how she'd been with me. Would she always be that way? Kind, gentle, and caring?

She'd even made my favorite soup, when I told her about it.

I could have it all, maybe. If I played this right. A beautiful resort here in South Carolina, a beautiful woman by my side, and something I'd never had from a woman before. Romantic love.

Alright, so that last part was my own fault. It wasn't that I blamed a woman for not loving me, but I'd built walls around my heart. Miss Stephanie had just smiled them all down was the problem. That smile of hers was infectious. It had been like a virus that infiltrated my heart and had slowly torn pieces out of that wall, until it was gone.

All that was left for me to do was to admit to myself that what I felt for her was far more than lust, or even affection. I cared for her. Deeply.

That shook me, as it always did, when I allowed myself to think about it. I wasn't the kind...

"It seems I am," I said to the empty room.

This could be my life, I thought: empty rooms, depressing quiet, and loneliness, if I played it all wrong. Or it could be the most wonderful thing I've ever experienced. Could I keep without losing my heart, though?

Or had I already lost that?

I turned the show off and ran my hands over my face. Music. Maybe that would help. YouTube opened, and the first item on offer was Bruce Springsteen's *I'm on Fire.* Fucking hell.

I scrolled past it and glared at the screen. I loved all genres and eras of music, but that song hit too close to the bone right now. I found some country music to play and tried to go back to writing up the contract. I had it out before the lawyer arrived and now took it back up.

It still looked like more of a letter than a contract, and I'd decided to leave it that way. I was on my third rendition of the thing and still didn't have it exactly right. I had a row of promises, a row of things I wanted from her, and a date at the end. There were two places to sign, my name and hers.

I went to my laptop and opened it. I found my writing program and opened that up.

I made nice, neat tables and filled them in then added some text.

It still read like a proposal, and that wasn't what I wanted. I wanted a contract. I went and found a copy of the old one on my laptop's hard drive and opened it. This was more like it. I started to edit things, took out the part about money altogether, left in the parts about privacy, and started to add in stuff from the new one. That just made it messy, and just as I thought I'd say fuck it and learn to live without the damned thing, Stephanie came home.

"Hi, babe," I called out and shut the laptop. I didn't want her to see the contract yet.

"Hey, Dylan. How are you, babe?" She

sounded tired, but there was an extra sadness there.

"Hey, what's wrong?" I took her hand, and she came to sit on my lap at the kitchen table.

"Nothing, just a few problems I have to deal with." She sank into me, her face warm against my neck. I felt a dampness too and wondered if she'd been crying.

"Anything I can help with?" I hugged her close and let her just relax into me. It felt good, even if my back did protest the extra weight.

"Not really, no. Just … stupidity." She kissed my cheek and got up. "I shouldn't be sitting on you with your back like that. How did your day go?"

She pulled her coat off, threw it in the bedroom, and came back to sit with me.

"Wine?" I asked and got up to get a glass for her and took a bottle from the fridge. I couldn't have it with my medicine, but I thought she needed some of it.

"Yes, please."

"My day went fine," I said once I sat. "The lawyer came. We got papers signed and stuff done. It looks good."

"I'm glad for you. I know you've waited a long time to get this settled." She sipped her wine then frowned. "What happens once you've found a place? Do you go back to Kansas?"

Ah, that question had finally occurred to her.

"I'll be here for a while. I want to get everything settled and opened, and then I'll figure out where to go next. I'm normally in Kansas or California, but I've neglected both a little lately. They'll need to be checked on soon, and the resort in Washington too." I blew air through my cheeks at the thought of all that travel. "I'll be here for a long time, though."

"Good," she said and finished her wine. "Are you hungry?"

"We can order out if you're tired? I don't want you to exhaust yourself."

"I'm fine. Besides, cooking soothes me." She brushed her fingers through my hair and smiled. "It reminds me of happy times."

"I'm surprised you know how to cook."

"Oh, why's that?" She looked confused, and I wondered if I'd broken one of our unspoken rules. Don't ask about my past, and I won't ask about yours.

"It's just, you seem well educated. Most of the time, people who spend so much time on education rarely know how to cook." Whew, hopefully I'd sidestepped that one.

"I spent summers at home, with the cook's daughter in the kitchen. I'd sneak down during the nights, and we'd cook up a storm." I saw a sweet expression cross her face as the memories replayed. Hmm, a live-in cook. She definitely came from money then.

Not that I was judging, but Stephanie was a mystery I wanted to untangle. Every now and then she'd give me a clue. I didn't want to tell my secrets, although she could look online and find most of them. They weren't actually secrets, just things I didn't want to talk about. She may have already done that, for all I knew. If she did, she hid it well.

She got up suddenly, a move that startled me. "Excuse me a minute. I'll, uh, I'll be right back."

I heard the tap go on in the bathroom and wondered. What had upset her so much? I was almost certain she was crying. I waited for her, and when twenty minutes had passed, I went to the door. "Stephanie?"

"I'm okay. I'll be out in a minute," she shouted, her voice strangled by tears.

"Let me in, babe." I held my hand to the door and turned the knob. She didn't protest, so I went in. She was sitting on the edge of the bathtub, a towel clutched to her face.

"Don't look at me," she said from behind the towel. I pulled that down and took her in my arms. Her face was red, her eyes were still streaming, and her nose was stuffed up.

"I won't look at you, but you're still beautiful, my darling. You don't have to tell me what's wrong. I know we both have our secrets, but let me hold you, at least."

"Nobody's ever … fuck!" She gripped at the panels of my shirt and sobbed deep and hard.

I'd break whoever had made her cry, as soon as I found out who it was. Had she been about to say nobody's ever held her while she cried before? I'd break her family too, if any of them were still alive.

Fucking bastards, to leave such a wonderful person out in the cold, with nobody to lean on when she cried. It occurred to me that maybe some of Stephanie's strength and stoicism came from never being loved properly.

"Have you never had anyone to hold you when you cried, babe?" I asked, breaking past my own barrier to invade her privacy.

"No, I've just, I've never, well, no." She kind of skated around an answer, before she finally just gave me a simple one. I pushed her hair back and looked at her in her watery gray, but still lovely, eyes.

"You do now." I picked her up and carried her to the bed, to our bed. "You were here for me when I needed you. I'll be here for you. Always."

I crawled into bed with her and held her until she fell asleep. She didn't sleep long, but she needed it. When she came back into the kitchen an hour later, I'd left the bed and had a simple meal on the stove. I put a pile of spaghetti on each plate and spooned some sauce she'd made and left in the freezer.

I was on my way back to the table when my left leg just gave out. It went totally dead, and I went down to my knees. I managed to save our dinner, but Stephanie and I stared at each other. I could feel the fear I knew I couldn't hide. It was reflected in her eyes.

"Dylan?" she asked softly. "What's wrong?"

She came and took the plates from me, and I leaned down to the floor. I moved around but could not get back up. My left leg was totally numb. Gradually, after a very long, terrifying wait, it came back to life.

"Sciatica, I guess. I'll, uh, I'll call my doctor tomorrow. It's fine now. Don't worry." I sat at the table and stared at my plate. I was too embarrassed to lift my eyes. I was also afraid to see pity there. I knew she would never be disgusted by any of this, but I knew she'd pity me. Pity might break me, and I wanted to avoid it, if I could.

"Let's eat. Really, I'm fine now." I'd have to wipe up the floor later, some of the sauce had hit the tiles, but it would wait. For now, I had to sort Steph out. She had enough to worry about without worrying about me.

There wasn't a lot that could be done for me. Which was one of the reasons I'd wanted a contract. I didn't want Stephanie to fall in love with a man who might not be around for the rest of her life. I took a deep sigh and ate a bite of my spaghetti. It wasn't worth worrying about, and the spill had reminded me of something I'd tried really hard to forget.

I wasn't a whole man. I wasn't completely sick, but I wasn't well either. Stephanie didn't need a burden in her life. I would become one eventually, and no young woman should be faced with that either.

No, it was back to the contract after tomorrow. Maybe back to the doctor too. We took a long swim in the pool after that and spent some time reminding each other why we were together. Stephanie had an amazing body, and she knew how to use it well. In the supportive weight of the water, it was easier to move too, and I managed to get us both where we wanted to go with little effort.

Later, after a shower and a kiss goodnight, I went back to my office and turned on my laptop. My symptoms were getting worse. I'd email the doctor and find out if he was worth the money I'd paid him. He wrote prescriptions for whatever I needed and sent them to whatever pharmacy I asked him to. His specialty was my problem and he knew travel wasn't the greatest thing for me, so he did as I asked.

I typed up an email, detailed what had happened, and fired it off to him. Not long after that, I got a reply. New medicine would be waiting for me at the pharmacy in the morning. Great, more medicine. I was hoping he'd tell me to increase one or the other that I was already on. Not add a new one in. Oh well, I decided. I might as well give it a try.

Chapter 15
Emily

Dylan was in his office, trying to get some work done. He wanted to let me sleep in peace, but I doubt I'd get much sleep tonight. Not any that was restful anyway. I'd checked my mail, before I came up to the apartment last night.

It was my habit to read the mail in my car before I went up, throw away what I didn't need and hide the rest under my car seat until I could deal with it or take it home. Dylan was rarely in my car, but I didn't want to leave mail in the glove box, just in case he checked in there for something. I didn't want him to go looking for a napkin and find a letter with my real name on it. I still hadn't figured out how to tell him that.

I'd been in a good mood, going through the stack of envelopes when one caught my eye. It was from my brother. I'd thought it was odd that he sent me a letter, rather than emailing me, but when I read the contents, I understood why.

My brother, the man who had been this demigod in my eyes, my whole life, had officially cut me out of the family. I was not to contact any of them, at any time, not even our parents. It was signed by my father and Trent.

I didn't know how he'd managed to get Dad to take his side on this, but he had. The rest of it was official documents, detailing how I'd still remain part of the family's business dealings, but my role was as a silent, unheard, totally ignored partner. I didn't exist, except for when it came to accounting details. I was no longer a member of the family.

I knew it, Trent had said those words to me, but I hadn't thought he'd go through with it. I thought he'd changed after he married and settled down. He'd become nicer, calmer, and much more loving. To the rest of the family, at least. Now, he thought I was a traitor and had disowned me. That cut me deeply.

I'd cried in the car but had stopped after a while. I didn't want anyone to see me crying like a baby in the parking garage, so I left the mail under my seat and went up to see Dylan. I'd tried to pretend everything was normal, but it wasn't. It was terrible!

I'd been comforted when he took me in his arms and tried to soothe me. Nobody in my life had ever done that for me. I couldn't even remember my mother doing it. Not even when I was a little girl. There'd been an occasional hand on my arm, or an arm around my shoulders, but I couldn't remember anyone ever hugging me to comfort me. Now, if they'd needed comfort, it had been totally different.

I'd always been there, ready with my ears to listen and my arms to hug. That had never been returned, which was one of the reasons I'd walked away in the end. I'd chosen Dylan over my family, and this was my punishment. I should have known it was coming. Trent had always been capable of a little cruelty. He thought I'd betrayed the family somehow, so of course, he'd turned into super-dick.

God, could I ever fix this? Did I want to? My family hadn't exactly been the greatest people in the world to me. My mother had always been consumed by her devotion to my father, and my brothers were the kind who treated me like a baby, or a nuisance, until they'd needed a babysitter. When I'd put a stop to that, I'd suddenly become this *thing* that they didn't understand.

Now, I was really, truly alone. Except for Dylan and Roxie. My best friend and the man who was my ... what? Lover? That just sounded silly to my often too pragmatic mind. He wasn't my partner any more than he was my boyfriend. He'd been my Mr. Dark when I'd first met him, and then my sir. Now, he was Dylan. A real human being and not just a fantasy.

Although, he did exceed my fantasies in many ways, which didn't happen often. Most of the time, when I imagined what someone would be like, they were far from my daydreams, or events just weren't as exciting as I'd imagined they would be. Dylan had brought fantasy to vivid life and had taken me well beyond those girlish daydreams. I just didn't know what to call him.

Now, as I snuggled down into my pillows, I tried to picture what life would be like in the future. No more noisy family gatherings or Christmas at the estate, that huge palace that my father owned. No more little faces looking up at me with happiness in their eyes when we played together. I wouldn't see the love and need for comfort from one of my nieces or nephews when they had a nightmare that woke them up.

I'd grown used to the noise of children and changing diapers. I laughed as I remembered just how many times I'd been peed on by baby boys. Even those times had made me smile, even though I'd been so lonely I could barely stand it. I'd have to find a way to fix all of this, eventually. Just as soon as I had settled things with Dylan. If we could settle it.

It wasn't just the contract, it was who I was. I just know he'll think I used him or that my family used me to get to him. That was the furthest thing from the truth, and at this point in time, all I wanted to do was run away from it all. That would mean leaving Dylan, and I couldn't do that. Not just because I'd come to need him as much as I needed air, but because something was wrong with him.

That pain he'd been having was getting worse, and he seemed to tire much earlier than he had just weeks ago. He wouldn't tell me what it was, and I had to respect his privacy for now. I kept my thoughts on Dylan, and eventually, despite my earlier thoughts that sleep would be impossible, fell into a peaceful dream.

The next day passed quickly. Dylan was out most of the day after lunch, and he didn't come home until dinnertime. I'd gone out to the grocery store, too antsy to use the delivery service, and had met up with Roxie for a quick coffee before she had to go home and get ready for work. She listened as I told her about the letter Trent had sent, and then she shocked me.

She put her hand over mine, squeezed it, and told me she'd be my family until Trent stopped being such a dick. It made my heart melt, and tears stung my eyes. I'd thanked her, and we'd both let the moment pass. It was easy to not feel so lonely now. Roxie and I had become friends the moment we met, but now, well, she really was almost like a sister to me.

She'd let me into a world I'd wanted to explore, and she'd been there to see me through it. Now, she'd see me through this too. I loved her for it, I really did.

I'd come back to Dylan's place after that and had chicken cooking in a wok to add to the salad I'd prepared beforehand. I needed something else to go with it, though.

"That smells delightful. What is it?" Dylan asked as he came up behind me. His arms slid around my waist to pull me back against him. I leaned my head back, and he kissed my neck.

"Just some grilled chicken for a salad. Do you want something to go with it?" I turned in his arms to look at him, happy in my role of housewife for the moment.

"Some of that French bread will go nicely with it, but I want to have you for dessert." He nuzzled into my neck and tickled me. I laughed as I pushed him away.

"Well, no dessert until you've had your dinner, my lord." I winked at him and turned back to the chicken. He was in a good mood, the kind that meant he'd wanted to be playful. I'd be in for a night of fun then.

He set the table, and we ate together quietly, but I kept looking up to see his eyes on me. There was desire there, and happiness, and I felt my body already responding to it.

"I think you should put that mask back on for me, Stephanie. There was something about fucking a woman whose face I couldn't see that just made me, well, really fucking hard."

"Anything you like, sir." I got up, cleaned the table off, washed up the few dishes we'd used, and went to sit in his lap. He pushed his chair back to make room for me and took me in his arms.

"Do you know how perfect you are, pet?"

His eyebrow quirked, a challenge added to his name for me.

Did I want to play, the name and the eyebrow asked. I slid down from his lap and settled on my knees in the floor. "You tell me I am, sir, so it must be so."

"Good answer. Go get your mask and get ready for me."

My nipples went tight, and I felt heat begin to pool between my thighs. I did love his games. Only, it wasn't always a game. Sometimes, every now and then, something inside both of us would flip, and the air around us would change. Times like now, when good moods instantly went from happiness to a need so strong, we couldn't break free from it.

I might be more than content with Dylan, but I still needed that strong hand that had drawn me to him in the first place. I went into the bedroom and looked around for my mask. It wasn't in my drawer where I usually kept it. I heard my phone go off and glanced at it. I had an alert of some kind, so I checked it.

I sat on the bed when I saw it. Ember, my other sister-in-law whose legal name was Bridget, had a new album out. Her greatest hits. I hit play on the video that accompanied the article. I'd only heard a few chords of it before I turned it off. A song about finding love in a gilded cage that you couldn't break free from. Ember sang about how sweet that love was and how fulfilling it could be.

Kind of like what I have with Dylan, I thought and felt my stomach twisted into a knot. I closed the video, put my phone down, and went to finish my preparations. I brushed out my hair, put on a black nightgown that Dylan had bought for me, and brushed my teeth.

By the time Dylan came in, a pair of black silk ropes in his hands, I was ready for whatever he wanted to give me. "Make me yours, Dylan."

"You know I will, Stephanie." He stripped

down to his dark gray trousers and joined me on the bed. "I'll wipe that sadness from your eyes, pet."

I gasped and looked up at him, my eyes wide with surprise. I thought I'd hid it, but now I knew I hadn't. "Thank you, sir."

"You can thank me later. Give me your hand." He held his right one out, so I gave him my right one. He tied that to a hook on the back of the headboard and then tied the other one. By that time, he was straddling me.

He looked down at me with heat in his eyes and leaned down close to my ear. I felt his chest press into mine, through the thin silk of my nightgown, and my nipples responded. His lips brushed at my neck and then just below my ear. I couldn't help it when I shivered with anticipation.

"You are so eager for my touch, Stephanie."

"Always, sir," I responded automatically, though it was the truth. I was always ready for him.

"Good girl. Now, help me roll you over." He'd added hooks in strategic places on the back of the headboard. He could spread my arms wide, which usually meant I couldn't move, or he could keep them close together and give me enough rope to turn and move around.

This time, I had just enough room to turn, but I'd have to cling to the headboard to stay up. I would also be forced to stay on my knees because relaxing onto my stomach would be too uncomfortable. Hmm, I thought, he wanted to distract me from my troubles. I wasn't about to change his mind.

I turned with his help and soon found myself on my knees, my feet spread apart, and my back arched high to rest my head on the headboard.

"Such a lovely round ass, pet." He moved up behind me and to the left a little. "It just needs a little color to make it prettier."

His hand came down, fingers tight together,

thumb tucked in, and so that when he slapped my ass it made more sound than sensation. The next slap he gave me was mainly with his fingers. That one had a little sting to it, and heat started to rise within me.

"Don't tease me, Dylan," I said, a moment of forgetfulness. Or was it?

I grinned when his fingers came down again, harder, on the other side of my bottom. "Don't sass, pet."

"I'm sorry, sir." I wasn't, especially when his hand came down harder, again, on the left side.

This time, the slap came with a warm palm to soothe the skin. He slid his hand around the red area that I knew must be there now, and the touch soothed the itch that came with the slap. I squirmed, the sting still not quite gone.

"Sir! I'm so sorry, I won't sass you anymore." It was only part of the game, and he knew it.

"Are you sure about that, my dear? I'm afraid I've had to tell you too many times now."

His voice was stern, and it sent a thrill straight through me.

His fingers dipped lower, down into the wet heat between me. Another slap, and this time I couldn't hold back a moan of pleasure. My sadness was gone now. There was only Dylan and the desire he made me feel.

Chapter 16

Dylan

I thought the sadness would be gone from her eyes when I came home earlier, but it was still there. If anything, it was worse. There was something defeated about the way her shoulders slumped ever so slightly. I still wanted to punch whoever it was that gave her that sadness, that took away some of the light of joy she always carried around with her.

Later, once I'd sent her into orbit more than a few times, I held her close to me. We were both still naked, and she breathed softly against me. I wanted to help her with whatever was wrong but wasn't sure I could.

"You know, if you need my help, I'm here for you, right? All things aside, Stephanie, I will never let you hurt or be afraid, if I can help it." I felt her tense in my arms, but I pulled her hips more tightly to mine and ran my left hand down her arm. "It's okay, I'm not going to make you tell me anything, or try to make you talk, but I do want you to know that I am here for you."

I paused, but she didn't speak. I knew she was awake, though. I could feel it in the way she breathed, a little quick and tense.

"You don't have to fight your battles alone. Not so long as you have me in your life." I paused again, but she still didn't answer.

I didn't think she was going to respond at all and was about to roll away to give her some space when she turned in my arms. Her warm, pliant body melded to mine, and I heard her breathe as she tried to control her emotions. The poor thing was tore all out of frame, and I wondered who she really was. Who could leave such a beautiful creature to fight her own battles like this?

I suspected she hadn't come from the same kind of past that I had. There was nothing about her that screamed impoverished childhood or lack of education. She seemed similar to my adoptive mother's younger female friends, well-spoken with an air about her that wasn't exactly superiority but was definitely regal.

That didn't mean she wasn't hurt while growing up. I'd found, in my experience, that a lot of these rich families saw their daughters as pawns, tools to showcase their own wealth and power. My adoptive parents obviously weren't like that, but some of the people they knew had left me gaping with their lack of care for their children. The boys were meant to go out and carry on the family name while the girls were to marry and produce children for their respective husband's family. It wasn't something that I ever quite grew used to.

She didn't cry now, or even speak, she just clung to me until she got her breath under control and had stopped trembling. I'd never seen her so shaken up, and while it made me feel good that she felt safe enough to show her vulnerability to me, it made me feel helpless. I didn't know who I had to kill for causing this, or how to make it better for her.

We had started this whole thing as a business transaction, but now here we were, all these weeks later, and she was all but sobbing in my arms. I had to wonder if she was attacked, but surely, I'd see signs of that? I knew every inch of her skin, and there wasn't a mark on it. Would all attacks leave marks? Or maybe something had been said to her verbally.

I didn't know, and for the first time, I hated the fact that we were so afraid to tell each other our secrets. If we could just be open and honest with each other, I'd know who needed to die right now. I knew most of the fact that we kept things from each other was my fault. It was how I'd wanted this relationship to be. I hadn't wanted a relationship, and I'd built these walls around us both, but the problem was, there was always a price to pay when you tried to cut yourself off from others.

Was this love? The need to protect, to make her smile again? Was that what love did to you? I didn't know. I knew about loving my parents, the people who took me in and gave me a real childhood and the real parents who had nearly destroyed me. I knew about loving a puppy or a kitten, pets. I didn't know a damned thing about romantic love.

Something that I wanted to smother with a pillow, deep inside of me, kept telling me she was the one, but I'd never wanted the one. I'd just wanted a pet to play with. She was that, but she was so much more than that. I'd tried to deny it for a long time, and even now, I tried to find reasons, any reasons, why this couldn't be love.

It was infatuation, which had to be what it was. It would pass eventually, right? I kept waiting for it to start to pass, this fascination with her, this need to be with her, but that wasn't what happened. Instead, it just kept getting stronger.

It was kind of scary, but I thought I could control it. I was starting to suspect I might be wrong. I wasn't a man who would deny himself, though, so if it happened, it happened. If this was love, then I guessed I had to get used to it because I knew one thing for sure. I didn't want to give her up. Not for anyone.

Her breath started to even out again, and I heard a soft snore at one point. When her body completely relaxed and she rolled away from me, I got out of bed, put my robe on, and headed to my office. I had new medicines I'd picked up at the pharmacy earlier. I wanted to do some reading about them.

I needed to know what the side effects were, how often I was supposed to take them, and what the benefits were supposed to be. I wasn't big on taking drugs, but I wanted to be around for a while longer, so if that was what it took, then I'd do it. *You want to be around for Stephanie*, a little voice said in the back of my mind.

I couldn't deny that part, at all. She made me want to live life to the fullest. That trip to the island and the one down to New Orleans had shown me that. I wanted to show her the places she'd never been, and I wanted to experience that joy with her. I wanted to experience life with her. If that meant taking medication, so be it.

I read the dosages and saw that it was time to take one of them. There were three new bottles. He wanted me to stop taking the one I was on and take these new ones instead. I took a deep breath and took the pill. The other two I had to take in the mornings.

I spent an hour or so researching each medicine and decided that the benefits outweighed the risks. It would keep me going, this new stuff. I hoped. I glanced at the door to my office. Stephanie needed me to be around. She'd said it herself, she'd never had anyone care about her, hug her, as I had the last couple of days.

Maybe it was time to let my guard down with her. I still wanted the contract, because I needed that wall between us, love or not. I needed to keep that distance there. I thought I was past the panic stage, where I just wanted to deny it completely and block her out, but I wasn't anywhere near the wedding bells and baby rooms stage. I needed to keep a level head, at all times.

I had the family business and my own side projects to think of. There were countless people depending on me to keep the businesses going. I had to protect that empire too. I couldn't make a rash mistake because I'd fallen for somebody. I had a lot of people depending on me to take care of myself and my actions.

Sometimes, times I wouldn't admit too very often, I wished I'd been given a different life. A normal one where my parents weren't the people they were, and that I'd had siblings. I'd have become a mechanic or maybe I would have become a business tycoon anyway, I was good at it, but I wouldn't have this constant pressure to be perfect, to be on top, always. Maybe I wouldn't have been so afraid of what it meant when I looked at Stephanie and my heart skipped a beat.

I pushed away from my desk with that thought. That was just a little too sappy, even for me, and I laughed softly at myself.

I glanced at the clock and saw it was late, or I'd have called my mom. She was probably up with my dad anyway, but I didn't want to disturb them. Late night calls were always stressful, even if the other person only wanted to talk. I'd leave it for another day then.

I pulled a stack of papers from my desk drawer and went through them. I found the ones I wanted, full of red ink and black writing, and read over it all again. I opened the file on my computer and began to make the edits I'd made on the paper copy. This would be our contract. I wanted her to read it first, before she said yes or no, because this wasn't the contract that I'd given her all those weeks ago.

This was something much different. It was a letter of love, in a sense. It held promises for the future, if our relationship lasted longer than six months, and it was an agreement that we'd try to be a little more open with each other. There were rules, of course, but nothing she hadn't already agreed to, and there were concessions if we wanted to change something in the contract.

Basically, it was me admitting that a contract wasn't exactly what we needed at this point in time. I'd started to see that happiness was within reach. I had it now, but I could have it for a lot longer, if I gave in to her way of thinking, just a little bit.

My past stood between us; I was big enough to admit that. She'd gone along with it because she had secrets of her own, but I knew she wanted that to end. She wanted to let go and tell me the things that bothered her, but she wasn't sure she should because I held her at arm's length in so many ways.

I'd have to trust Stephanie, and I wasn't sure I could. Not because she wasn't worthy, but because I'd always found that the hardest thing to do in life. If anybody deserved loyalty and trust, it was Stephanie. Something always held me back.

The image of my mother's face flashed in my mind, my real mother's, that night that she tried to erase us all from the world. She'd looked insane ... she'd looked like she loved me. Then she'd poured gasoline all over my carpet to kill me. It was pretty hard to trust anyone after that. I didn't think there was a person alive who could think it would be easy to trust after your own mother tried to kill you.

Stephanie's face had started to replace that faded memory, and that, more than anything, told me she was special. It wasn't just the sex, or that she let me spank her when I got the urge; she cared for me. I could see it in the way she talked to me, the way she made me forget my troubles, the way she tried so hard to give me everything I needed.

She'd even bought me jewelry. Not as a show of wealth or as a silly token, but to show me I mattered. I stared down at the ring on my middle finger, where it had been since the day she gave it to me. It had become part of my identity, that token of affection.

I'd been surprised when she gave it to me, a little shocked even. I'd never worn jewelry because I'd never been given any, and it never really occurred to me to go out and buy some for myself. It just wasn't something I'd ever wanted.

Stephanie's ring, the necklace, and the cufflinks, were special. Just like her.

I printed out the final version of the contract I wanted her to sign and put it back in my desk drawer. I'd take it out on the day our current agreement was up and give it to her. This one should make her happy.

I knew she'd avoided the matter and had changed the subject more than once, but this one was different. I thought she'd see the main promise in the whole thing, if she would just sit down and read it all. This wasn't a business contract. It was a promise that I'd try.

I knew it was probably stupid to offer her so much when I didn't know what my future held. I might not have many years left to give her, but right now, everything in me said I wanted to spend those years with her. I'd do my part, see my doctor, take the medicine, do whatever I could to hold off the inevitable, but I'd try. That was all I could do.

Now, I just had to get her to sit down and read it without getting angry and storming off. I could understand her viewpoint; she'd explained herself pretty well that night she'd walked out on me. I'd had a hard time admitting it then, but now, I could see. Stephanie was lonely, and with me she'd found a measure of happiness. She wasn't so lonely anymore. She didn't want to give that up, and the contract was a threat to that happiness, she thought.

This one wasn't. It was a concession, and a hope that we could get to a different level together. I couldn't make too many promises, but I could start out small. I'd offer her a relationship and in a few months, we'd re-examine where we were. If things were going well, and if we wanted to make changes, we would. That was as much as I could offer. Anything else might be a lie.

Chapter 17
Emily

We had one more day together, and then I suspected my fine Mr. Dark would emerge with a dreaded contract for me to sign. I wasn't so sure now, he'd changed in the last couple of weeks, but I had a feeling he had something up his sleeve. I'd seen him working on something, more than once.

He'd always put it away before I could see exactly what it was, and that was what made me suspicious. He didn't want me to see what he was working on because he didn't want to

Dark Secret

upset me. The thing was, right now, I'd take whatever he had to offer.

After breakfast that morning, Dylan went off to do some things he needed to do, and I went back home. I did some dusting, took care of the mail, and looked around the place. I had projects I hadn't worked on sitting out on the kitchen table, and there were clothes in the dryer that needed to be ironed now if I ever wanted to wear them in public.

I was glad I hadn't bought any potted plants; the poor things would have died from neglect by now. I spent far more time at Dylan's than I did here now. It was here that I could finally sit and listen to Ember's new song without fear of being caught. Not that Dylan would ask me to explain listening to a pop star sing, but it would make me feel funny.

I kicked off my Louboutin heels and settled on the couch. I started my laptop and clicked icons until I was on the video for Ember's song.

255

The official video wasn't out yet, but the record label had released the song. I knew her story, her real story, better than the public did. She'd had a rough life, a very rough life, and had been given the unfortunate name of Bridget, when her father's last name was Jones.

When she'd met my brother, she'd been using a name that she had decided to use as her stage name: Ember. It was how most of us knew her, but I'd heard my brother, her husband, affectionately call her Bridge more than once. It was their thing, so I'd left it alone.

Her song was beautiful. Like most of her music, it reached right into my soul and bared the things I hid even from myself. Things like how much I missed my family, the babies, and my sisters-in-law. I'd wanted some space of my own when I'd walked away all of those months ago. I'd wanted to have my own identity.

Somehow, that had turned into me being banished from the family entirely. I wasn't sure how, or why, but it had happened. I was the one, as always, left to pick up the pieces. I was sure Jessi had probably made Trent's life hell since he'd made that decision, but then, I remembered that she'd forgotten my birthday too. That might be the one that hurt the most.

We'd been so close, up until my brother finally realized he loved her. Then he'd become her world. The babies came along, and well, I'd become an unpaid babysitter, the family nanny. She wasn't a snob now, it wasn't that, it was just that she was consumed by her love for my brother and the family they'd made together. I couldn't really blame her for that, even if it did hurt to be left behind.

Trent wouldn't understand that, and he wouldn't understand what it was like to be a blip on the family's radar. None of my brothers would, I guessed. They were all big, bad, Alpha males and always had been. They'd been trained by our parents to expect me to take care of them. I always had, until I'd had enough.

I didn't think it was too selfish to want something for myself, some happiness, but apparently it was. My brother had taken a dislike to Dylan, for some idiotic reason, and that had destroyed any chance we'd had for reconciling after I walked away. I'd wanted to give them time to understand that I meant something more to them than a secretary or nanny would. Then Trent had seen me with Dylan, and he'd made assumptions.

I guess he'd told Dad those assumptions, because even he'd turned his back on me. My father, always so practical, would have taken the advice of his firstborn, even though it was me who always went along with his schemes. Even though it was me who took care of him when he needed me.

I closed the video screen and stared at nothing. I had to get past this all, somehow. My family had abandoned me. It was a tough pill to swallow, but I'd have to. I'd been ordered not to contact any of them. I wasn't sure what Trent would do if I did, but I knew his temper. It wouldn't be pretty.

I'd leave them alone, even if I did want to call Ember and congratulate her. Even if I did want to call Jess and check on the children. I would leave them all alone. So what if it made me sob when I thought about the fact that the children would forget about me? So what if they might one day ask who that lady is in the pictures with them, and they'd be told she was who, nobody?

I swiped at my tears and decided then and there that I'd sign Dylan's contract. It wasn't just because I'd be alone otherwise; it was because he had shown me love, even if he didn't want to call it that. He offered me far more than they ever had. He offered me a life to live, where they offered me mediocrity and spinsterhood.

I wiped my face dry and went into the bathroom to clean myself up. I'd had a good cry, but, honestly? I felt better for it.

Dylan had tried so hard to be what I needed last night. He'd distracted me when I was on the verge of breaking into tears, and he held me when that overwhelming grief came back. Because it was grief, this pain. They weren't dead, but they might as well have been, if Trent had his way. They'd cut off contact and ordered me to back off.

I was grieving and probably would for a while. The good news was, I thought as I reapplied mascara, I had a new life just waiting on me to have the guts to take it. I stepped back when I was done, saw that my eyes were still a bit red, but I didn't look so deathly now. Yep, it was time to greet this new life with both hands at the ready.

Dylan had already said we were going out that night, but he hadn't said to where. I went through my closet, found a long sleeved dress of brown knit cashmere, and put it in a bag to carry back to Dylan's. The dress looked like a really long sweater, it came down to my calves, but it was form fitting and had a deep, plunging neckline. Sexiness wrapped in innocent cashmere, he'd love it. I hadn't worn it out yet, but I knew it would turn heads.

I picked out a pair of brown suede leather ankle boots with spike heels and added some jewelry to a smaller bag I'd put in my purse. If it wasn't the right dress to wear, I'd pick out something I had at his place. I found my black leather jacket, perfect for the cool nights at the beach, a brown and white wraparound scarf, and gathered up everything.

For a moment, as I stood in the doorway, I wondered why we didn't come back here more often. Dylan was comfortable at his place, and this place was so new to me it didn't quite feel like home. I wondered if it ever would, and I kind of hoped it wouldn't. It would mean I'd found a home with Dylan if I wasn't here.

I closed the door, made sure it was locked, and walked away from the house with a smile on my face. An hour ago I'd been on my couch, crying my eyes out, but now, I was headed for a new life. I hoped.

I got back to his place after a meeting for the charity group, where I saw Roxie, and I put my bags down. Yes, this place felt more like home than my own home did. I kicked off my shoes, picked them up to put them in the closet space he'd set aside for me, and hung up my dress. It wouldn't wrinkle, but I wanted it up anyway.

I went into the kitchen, made myself some lunch, and then relaxed on the couch for a bit. I was feeling a little tired after all of this crying and emotional upheaval. I didn't mean to fall asleep, but realized I had when Dylan came in.

"Hello, sleeping beauty. Do you want to wake up, or shall I cancel our plans for the night?" he asked, concern written all over his face.

"Oh no, don't cancel! I was just a little tired, that's all. Let me get up and get dressed." I smiled and kissed him quickly before I got up to run to the bathroom. "How long do we have before we have to be there?"

"A couple of hours, babe. Don't rush. Come here." He pulled me down to him, and we fell together on the couch, laughing.

This is what I'd gained for my troubles. A man tickling me into laughter, until I protested that I'd pee all over us both if he kept it up. A man who adored me, from what I could tell. "Stop, Dylan, or we'll end up in bed and forget these plans of yours."

"No! Get off me, woman! Shoo!" He pushed at me playfully until I moved away and sat up, completely prim and proper now. "My plans must not be foiled. Go, clean yourself and make yourself worthy."

He'd put on a very bad English accent and some very hoity-toity airs, which he finished off with an imperial wave of his hand. Oh indeed. Playful, was he?

I could swear he even patted at his hair a bit as I walked away.

An hour later, I emerged from the bathroom, my hair clean and curled in soft waves around my shoulders and down my back, makeup perfectly in place, and my own special scent, a French perfume that had been designed for only me in Paris at a very exclusive boutique, to finish off the picture I'd created. Soft innocence, but an underlying note of alluring seduction. Dylan would love it.

"Perfect," he breathed as he inhaled my perfume. "God, I do love that scent, what is it?"

"Just something my mother found for me when I was a teenager. Are you ready to go?" I looked at him. He was in a fresh suit, charcoal gray with very faint black pinstripes. Beneath it he wore a black silk shirt and a tie that matched his suit. "You look very nice."

"So do you, babe. I'm ready if you are." He took my hand, kissed my knuckles softly, and led me from the apartment.

He drove us out of North Myrtle Beach and into Myrtle Beach, the commercialized side of the Grand Strand, where the boardwalk stretched along the beach for miles, ice cream parlors and novelty shops lined the streets on both sides, and families crowded the streets as they rushed from one attraction to the next, enjoying their vacation. Before long he pulled into a very nice looking restaurant and took me inside. The place was elegant with a lot of black and white, the main colors for the décor. It wasn't too busy, but each table was arranged to give some privacy to the clients. We were in a corner that was very private, and a candle lit the area around our table.

"Oh, this looks nice." I sat and took the menu the waiter gave me.

"I hope so. It comes highly recommended." Dylan looked off to the left where the glass panes looked out on a very high resort and smiled. There was something secretly pleased about that smile, and it made me wonder. He didn't say anything, so I let it go.

The waiter soon took our orders and

brought us both a glass of white wine. We'd finished the meal before I knew it, and Dylan asked if I wanted dessert, or if I wanted the rest of our night to continue.

"This wasn't it?" I asked, surprised.

"No, not at all." He gave me a conspiratorial wink that was just a bit cheeky, and I couldn't help but smile with him.

"Go on then, tell me. What's the rest?"

"You'll have to wait and see." Another wink, and we were soon out of the restaurant and on our way somewhere else.

The next stop was a rather upmarket club. Only this one served cocktails that cost more than some people earned from their weekly paycheck, and the dancing was formal, ballroom style. Not the pounding, grinding music and dance of the place we'd met then. I smiled, excited at what he'd sprung on me.

I'd done ballroom dancing, I'd had it drilled into my brain, but it was usually reserved for charity balls and fundraisers at my father's golf club. This was new.

We had a drink, and talked about our day before we headed out to the dance floor. Dylan, yet again, impressed me with his dance skills. He led me through the moves expertly, and it was a night that would imprint itself on my brain forever.

Not even the fact that we got a flat tire on the way home could dim my happiness that night. I'd expected he'd call someone to come and help us, but he pulled off the side of the road, got out, and started pulling things out of the trunk like he knew what he was doing. We laughed together on the interstate as he showed me how to change a tire, then we got back on the road. It was cold, and I could have stayed in the car, but I didn't want him on the side of that road without me keeping an eye out for him.

It was late when we got home, and we laughed as we got into bed together. We were still laughing as he began to make love to me, and I couldn't have asked for a better day than we had. It was our last under our agreement, and I could only hope this was a sign of things to come. If he gave me such a perfect last day together, that could only mean even better things were on the horizon. Right?

Chapter 18

Dylan

I woke up the next morning and started the coffee and put some Danishes in the oven to heat up for breakfast. It wasn't the healthiest breakfast, but I needed to get out early this morning. I'd worn my little princess out the night before, so I went in to wake her up once everything was finished.

I'd have left her to sleep, but this was a special day. The day when we started something new. She woke up slowly and wrapped her arms around my neck once she realized I hovered over her. She clung to me tightly, and I knew she was perfectly aware of what today was. I ran my hands down her back and pulled her tightly to my chest.

"It's alright, Stephanie. It will all be over soon. Come with me. Let's have breakfast, and then I have to get to work." I kissed the side of her head and got up. I couldn't help the smile that spread over my face when I looked down at her.

She was still naked, and her body was ready for me, it always was. Not this morning, though. I had things to do, preparations to make. I'd finally got around that bastard Trent Thompson and ownership of one very beautiful resort was within my grasp. If I could get Stephanie to sign the contract today, life would be perfect.

She slid on a pink fleece robe and followed along behind me. Her hair was all over the place, and she had no makeup on, but I thought that might be one of the reasons I found her so incredibly sexy in the mornings.

She was unguarded, and there was no protective layer. It was just her and nothing else.

I put the plate of sweet treats on the table and filled her coffee cup, added a little bit of cream, and set it in front of her. I walked around and ate my own as I got ready to leave for the day. Once I finished, I washed my hands, dried them, and went to the other counter, where I'd left the contract.

"I have to go, but I want you to have a look at this." She looked up at me with stricken eyes, eyes that didn't want to face this so early in the morning. "It's not as bad as you think. I want you to read it carefully, sign it, and bring it back to me tonight, okay?"

She just continued to stare at me, and I felt a little niggle of worry. "If you don't come back, I'll know you didn't want to sign the contract, and that we're done. I don't want that, but if you can't face what I put in there, then... well, it's better if we end it now, before either one of us gets too hurt."

"Dylan…," she started, but I held a hand up to stop her.

"No. Just …, just read it, babe. I'll be back this evening, and if you're here, then we can talk, alright?" I leaned down, kissed her now sweet lips, and left her there.

I thought she'd sign it, if she bothered to actually read it. It was a masterpiece, in my mind. All she had to do was give it a chance and read it.

I went through the rest of my day without any major problems coming up. All I could think about was going home to Stephanie, however. Even when I took one final step to making my dreams of owning a resort on this coast, I couldn't stop thinking of her. She was always on my mind, though, and when I saw a jewelry store as I passed my lawyer's office, I stopped in.

"Can I help you, sir?" A small, punctilious

looking man came from behind a closed door. The smell of microwaved spaghetti sauce told me I'd interrupted the man's lunch. I'd best make it worth his while then.

"I'd like a necklace please." I told him as I came up to shake his hand. "Something in platinum, if you have it."

"Of course, sir, this way please." He showed me to a well-lit case, full of beaming metal and sparkling gems. "What is that dark stone, there in the heart-shaped pendant?"

"Ah, that is alexandrite, sir. A very good choice as it's very popular with the ladies now." He took the necklace out to show me how it changed color from red to green, and I had him set that one to one side. With the diamonds around the outer heart later, it was a bit showy.

Stephanie had started to wear brighter colors, and she had come out of her shell a bit since I'd first met her. She didn't wear flashy jewelry, but what she wore was always expensive and tasteful. The alexandrite would be for those days when she felt like showing off.

A few minutes later he pulled out a double heart necklace, formed from one piece of metal that intertwined around itself to form the two hearts and a lover's knot, as he called it. Just a piece of metal twisted into an intricate knot pattern, but still they both caught my eye. "I'll take both"

"Certainly, sir. All very good choices, anything else?" The man was on a roll, but I was finished with looking at jewelry. I wanted to get home and get the place ready for her. It wasn't Valentine's or an anniversary, but I did want the place to be romantic when she got there.

I stopped at a florist, picked up a variety of pink, white, and red roses, bought some candles that they had handy, and went home. The cleaner had been in, although there was very little for her to do except dust and wipe down the surfaces. I didn't know what time

Stephanie planned to be back, so I went to work right away.

I placed the candles throughout the house and decided I'd light them around five. She knew I was usually finished for the day around that time, so I figured she'd come back around then. The rose petals I sprinkled throughout the apartment and on the bed. A little cliché, perhaps, but I thought it was a nice touch.

After I finished that, I went into the kitchen and started to prepare some dinner. She liked paella, so I started to prepare the ingredients for the traditional Spanish paella that she liked the most. She wasn't always a fan of seafood, so I changed the recipe I'd learned and left those out.

It would take around an hour to prepare it all properly, so I turned the small television on in the kitchen to a music channel that actually played music, and started. I chopped up all the vegetables and the sausage, as well as some prosciutto, by the time a news report came on.

I wasn't really paying attention to it, it was just news about the music industry, and I was more concerned about which step of the preparation I was on than who'd put out a new album.

I turned to the island just behind the gas stove to pick up the tomatoes and glanced at the television. The woman on the screen was reporting about a new album from one of Stephanie's favorite singers, a woman who called herself Ember. The reporter went on to talk about how Ember was married to the hotel tycoon, Kevin Thompson, Trent Thompson's brother, and my blood went cold. That bastard again. I was about to turn away, but the pictures changed, and I stopped dead in my tracks. It couldn't be?

A picture had flashed on the screen, and I'd stepped closer, but the screen was too small. I went into the living room, the paella forgotten.

I turned on the television, punched in the number of the channel, and then backed up the program with the remote. I paused it when I saw the picture on the screen all over again. It was Stephanie. A slightly younger version of Stephanie, but there she was, holding a baby while Kevin and Ember embraced for the camera.

She stood just behind the couple, Stephanie's face beamed as happily as the other two and I just ... I just couldn't believe it. She knew Trent Thompson? How? My stomach was tight, and I felt slightly sick. The smell of the food didn't help, so I went into the kitchen and turned the stove off before I went to grab my laptop from the office.

When I sat on the couch in the living room, my eyes automatically went to the picture still paused on the screen. Now that I was looking, I could see a resemblance between Trent and Stephanie, and that made the muscles around my heart contract, until I let a very real pain in my chest. Surely it couldn't be?

A woman from a family like that had shown up at a strip club, looking for a dom? I thought about the observations I'd made in the past few weeks. How I'd thought that Stephanie was from a wealthy family, that she was obviously from a different class than most of the women who showed up at Elmo's, the club where we'd met. She'd always been so regal, I supposed was the right word. An air that one usually only gained when you came from money and had spent some time at a private school, or even boarding school.

My mind just couldn't process it all, and I looked down at my laptop. The thought struck that I could find out quite easily if Trent Thompson had a sister or not. His sister-in-law's hard-luck story told me that Stephanie wasn't her sister, but, maybe...

There was one way to find out.

I opened the laptop and clicked on the browser. I typed in Trent's name, the word family, and found a Wikipedia page, along with a slew of news reports and magazine articles about the man. It would seem women across the globe found the man irresistible, but that wasn't what I was looking for. I clicked the Wikipedia link. No, Wikipedia wasn't exactly the height of academic accuracy, but it was a place to start.

It was also the place that shattered my heart and the fragile bond of trust I'd given to Stephanie. Or, Emily, as it would seem her real name was.

Emily Thompson, aged twenty-six, was the youngest sibling of the Thompson brothers and youngest child of their father. There in black and white was all the evidence, the secrets she'd kept, and the instrument of my doom.

I'd been fucking a Thompson. Which could only mean she'd been sent to me to spy. Or that was what I thought when my brain finally started to function again. I went through Facebook, Instagram, Twitter, and a few other social media sites, and found pictures of her, always in the background. She was always pictured with a child in her arms once the Thompson brothers started to reproduce.

I scanned the images with eyes that wanted to find some difference, a mole that wasn't there in the pictures, or a change in eye color that would say that Emily wasn't Stephanie, that the woman I'd thought I was falling in love with wasn't a conniving bitch. The face changed, and sadness took over where the happiness had once shone. I didn't really notice that, though. I just noticed how Stephanie was undoubtedly Emily.

I sat there, stunned, unable to move. I couldn't see her wall on Facebook, she had that locked down, and her other social media had kind of tapered off more than a year ago, but I could tell it was her. There was rarely any conversation from her posts, and most of the time, there were no likes, shares, retweets, whatever people called that stuff. It wasn't something I was interested in.

It was obvious she'd had nobody to talk to,

and that she'd been posting to a world that didn't care that she existed. Even when she spoke about one of her nieces or nephews, she rarely got a comment or a like for it. No wonder she'd seemed so lonely.

The question now was, had she been lonely enough to give so much to me to spy on me? I could see Trent, that fucking bastard, ordering his sister to do whatever it took to get information out of me. I still couldn't understand his dislike of me, but if my suspicions were true then it was more than dislike. The man wanted to do whatever it took to keep me out of his playground. That was hatred.

I didn't understand it. I hadn't done anything to him, and a little competition could be healthy, but yet, the man still couldn't stand me. Which made me wonder how he could send his sister off to fuck the secrets out of a man like me. He obviously didn't care about her, or he wouldn't have used her like that.

I couldn't move after a while. I just stared between the television screen and the laptop screen. My Stephanie was actually Emily. A woman whose own family seemed to care little for her. My brain whirled, and remembered little snippets of thoughts. There'd been very few articles about her, and even her Wikipedia page was just a branch of Trent Thompson's page.

Daughter of, sister of, no marriages or education to report. Not that I doubted Step … I meant Emily was educated. She obviously was, but there'd been no interest in her life, so there'd been no need to fill in her details.

My thoughts warred with each other in my head. One side of me pitied the woman who had been so ignored by her own family, while the other was filled with rage. I'd been had, there was no doubt about it. Truly, totally had by the Thompson family.

I didn't want it to be true, but why else would a woman like her show up in a place like that? Had Roxie been in on it, I wondered. I could just imagine a man like Trent going to a place like that. I bet he was a regular in that downstairs dungeon, beating on subs until their bottoms were black and blue.

That made me shiver, because that meant that Trent and I had something in common. Not the beating part, but the domination part. Had he been there the night I first took Stephanie, Emily, to a private room to get to know her better? Had he sent her on her way with a kiss on her cheek and a pat on the head?

She was so eager to please that night, and I'd just taken it as part of the respect a dom was due. Had I been duped?

I thought about those innocent gray eyes that had looked up at me from the floor where she knelt, and rage filled me. I'd been had, by one very talented spy.

Chapter 19
Emily

I couldn't even call after Dylan when he left me this morning. If he had waited a minute, I'd have signed his contract without even looking at it. It wasn't worth the worry, the stress, or the arguing to me. All I wanted, all I needed was him, and I'd take him contract or not. He'd left, though, and here I was, alone with the thing.

I picked it up but didn't read it before I put it back down. I'd read it later, once I'd come back from the day I had planned. I shoved it in my bag after I got dressed, pulled out my car keys, and headed down to my car. I had a full day planned.

A woman wasn't born smooth, and I subjected myself to a full wax treatment before I headed to the hair salon. I wanted a darker tone added to my hair and a new cut. Nothing radical, I liked the length of my hair, but I wanted to be more … windswept, I guessed was the word. More romantic than practical.

By the time I'd had a few layers of skin removed and had my hair done, I was kind of tired. I went for lunch and managed to build up some energy for the rest of the day. I went to a few exclusive boutiques before I found exactly what I wanted.

A long, black, satin nightgown with silver threads shot through the black lace of the top of the gown. The satin shimmered and was as soft as melted butter to the touch. That went into the arms of the woman who had come out to greet me and asked if I'd needed assistance.

I added a new corset, black of course, with silver embroidery, and new stockings, a garter belt, and the most beautiful pair of panties.

They were less panties and more like a decoration for my lady bits, but I loved them. The front was a small triangle of black lace with a metal heart ring above the point of the triangle. Stretchy black lace was looped around the heart to create a waistline and near the bottom of the triangle to go around my lower hips and legs. The back was basically an invitation to spank me, or fuck me, because there was no crotch in these panties. Just ribbons of lace that fanned out from another heart ring in the back. I bought several pairs in different colors, because they were just luscious, and I couldn't resist.

There'd be no way Dylan could resist giving me a good spanking with those on. I was grinning by the time I found a bra with similar details, and I couldn't wait to get back to his apartment. For most of my life, I'd been practical. Pretty little things like the panties would catch my eye, but I'd had nobody to wear them for. Until the night I decided to change my fate. I'd bought some of the frilliest things I could find for that night.

Now that I knew Dylan, and knew him better, I had an eye for what might tickle his fancy. Although, me naked seemed to work well, I thought with a silent smirk of a laugh. I still hadn't read the contract, but I didn't need to. It would have the same lines in it, with another month or three added to it, and that would be that.

The sales woman showed me a few more things, then she took me upstairs to show me some dresses. I found the perfect dress for tonight there, a black bodycon dress that was backless, long sleeves, and the hemline hit me at mid-calf. Panels were cut out on the side of the skirt and along the arms with black ribbons added for a lace-up effect. It called my name, and I added that to my growing list of purchases.

I had the perfect pair of black Hermès Rumba sandals at home to go with that dress. I made my purchase and then drove home to finish my preparations. I showered, did my hair and makeup again, and then started to dress. I started to feel sexy the moment I put the bra and panties on. When I wiggled into the dress and closed the clasp at the back of my neck to keep the top panel up, I felt even more confident in myself. I added the beautiful set of shoes and stood to have a look in the mirror.

I was going to knock his socks off. I wanted to bite my lip, but I'd added the pale pink lipstick that he loved the most to my lips and didn't want to mar it. I controlled the old habit and looked at myself. A year ago I wouldn't have recognized the confident, beautiful woman in the mirror as me. I'd have said she was a model, maybe, or some socialite who had a clue about how to look like a sexy woman.

Yet, here I was, put together and lovely, even if I thought so myself. It was okay for a woman to think she looked good every now and then, right? And tonight, I looked damn good. I gave myself a sexy wink in the mirror, laughed, and left the house. It was a little difficult to drive with the heels on, so I put on a pair of flats I kept in the car, just in case, and pulled out of my driveway.

I glanced over at my purse and realized I still hadn't signed the contract. I'd sign it in the parking garage, I decided, and hit the gas as the light in front of me changed to green. Just a few more minutes, and I'd be in his arms again. I hadn't dared to dream that this could happen to me, but I'd taken a step, and a step had turned into another one, until I'd finally come to this point. I was about to plunge into a new world with Dylan, and I couldn't be more excited about it.

I pulled into the parking garage and parked before I took out the contract and fished around in my bag for a pen. When I found one, I flipped to the back page, signed the space left blank across from Dylan's signature, and slid the papers back into the bag.

I checked my makeup, wiped at the corners of my mouth to smooth the line of my lipstick, and got out. I'd put on a long, black wool peacoat to wear in the brief moments I was in the cold air, but I took it off once I made it inside the elevator. The ride up felt like forever as I counted the floors. About halfway up I looked in the mirror, straightened the top of my dress, combed out my hair with my fingers, and tried to figure out why I was so nervous. There was no need to be, yet, here I was with butterflies in my tummy.

Maybe it was because I'd decided that I would tell Dylan who I was tonight. I wanted my secrets out of the way, so they wouldn't plague me with guilt anymore. I knew he wanted me in his life, and from the tender moments we'd had together, I believed he was really starting to care about me. I wasn't so afraid to tell him who I was now, and I knew that would take a great weight from my shoulders.

I smiled when the elevator came to a stop with a ding, and the doors opened. Show time. I walked into the hallway, twisted my dress into just the right position, flicked away a speck of white fluff, and took a deep breath. With a pounding heart, I opened the door. The faint smell of paella greeted me, and that made my heart melt. He'd cooked for me.

He'd cooked before, but this told me he knew tonight was special too. It was my favorite dish, and he'd learned to cook it for me, just the way I liked it. I stepped in and closed the door behind me.

"Dylan? I'm back," I called out, but nobody answered. I spotted the rose petals on the floor, and my eyes went round with surprise. Oh my...

I hung my coat on a coat rack just to the left side of the door and put my bag there too. I took the contract out and saw that my hands were shaking. He still hadn't answered, but I could see the door to his office was closed. He might be on a call. I followed the path of the rose petals and stopped at the table in the hallway. Something glittered and caught my eye.

I saw two necklaces in black velvet boxes, all lined up. It was as if he couldn't decide which he'd liked best, so he'd bought both. My right index finger smoothed over each one, but it was the knot necklace that caught my eye. Simple, elegant, but so evocative of our relationship. We truly were twisted and knotted around each other, in so many ways. The knot looked complicated, but closer inspection showed it was very simple, also like our relationship in more ways than one.

I left the necklaces there when I saw there were candles on the table that hadn't been lit. It would seem I'd come back before he expected me to. I went into the kitchen and that was when something started to bother me. The tomatoes and other vegetables in the pan had gone cold. He wasn't preparing a meal; he'd stopped for some reason.

I'd left my phone in my bag, and that was on the coat rack in the hallway, but I knew he hadn't called me to say he had to go out. I'd have heard it because I left the sound up loud, just in case. No, he must be here. Why had he stopped cooking? Had something gone wrong?

I saw that he had a music channel playing on the television in the kitchen, but that was no kind of clue. It just meant that whatever had happened had been a surprise. A feeling of doom started to prickle at the back of my neck, and I glanced at the television. There was nothing that came on there that could have caused this, surely?

"Dylan? Where are you? What's wrong?"

Maybe he'd become ill. Maybe that was why he wasn't responding.

My heart flew into my throat, or so it felt, and started to pound in my ears as I made my way to the bathroom, fear a sudden and galvanizing force. I flew to the bathroom, his name on my lips, my eyes wide with fright, but the room was dark. I flicked on the switch and saw it was empty. Relief flooded through my veins, and I made my way further back to the bedroom.

"Dylan?" He wasn't in there either. I saw more candles and an amazing amount of rose petals on the bed, which really was romantic, but my heart didn't calm yet. Something was definitely wrong. I sat on the bed, certain that he was gone and wasn't in the house.

Where could he have gone? Oh! I know! I bet he had to go out for something for the paella. I bet he forgot something and had to rush out to get it. That must be what it was.

Relief flooded through me, and I sighed happily. Okay, crisis averted.

I waited on the bed for a few minutes, but he didn't come in, so I decided to open a bottle of wine to have it ready for when he got back. I went into the kitchen, opened a bottle of Spanish wine, and poured it into two glasses. He shouldn't have it if he'd had his pain medicine, but if he had, I'd drink it.

I carried the glasses out of the kitchen and into the living room. It was a miracle I didn't drop those glasses, because it scared the fuck out of me when I looked up to see him sitting there on the couch. I wasn't expecting him to be there, and I laughed at my own stupidity.

"God, Dylan, you scared the fuck out of me," I said with a bemused laugh. "Why didn't you answer me?"

Then, my eyes drifted to the television, and I saw the picture. Ember, so happy and in love, with Kevin and Trent as she left the awards ceremony where she was given album of the year by a very prestigious group. There, in the background where I always was, stood me with one of their babies in my arms.

I could have said it wasn't me, that I looked alarmingly like the woman in the picture, but I was done hiding who I was. I was Emily Thompson, not the Stephanie I'd become. Oh, my new self-confidence, my sense of worth, had all been built because of my fake persona, but underneath that name, I was the woman he thought I was. I just happened to be a little more than the stripper he'd taken me for when I first met him.

He didn't say anything, not then. Instead, he turned the laptop screen to me and flicked through browser tabs. That pitiful Wiki page, my Facebook page, the pitiful Instagram and Twitter I'd tried to maintain, as a wishful link to the outside world for so long. I'd barely ever raised anything more than a single like on most of my posts, but I kept hoping that one day I'd have a friend, or even a family member, who paid some kind of attention to my life.

It hadn't happened. Instead, I now had no family, at all, and it looked like the only man I ever wanted to spend my life with had found out my secret in the most horrible way possible.

"Do you care to explain this, Stephanie? Or do you prefer Emily? Miss Thompson, perhaps? Miss-you-are-Trent-Thompson's-sister even? Hmm?" I looked at his face, full of hurt, accusations, and rage.

I froze in place. All of my dreams had just been washed away. My plans for the perfect night, my hopes for our future, all of it, had just spoofed away in a barely visible cloud of smoke. I didn't know what to say or how to make this better. I'd hidden it for so long and had a thousand reasons why I had. The accusation in his eyes, the one that screamed I'd lied to him, told me that any answer I gave wouldn't be enough. If I tried to say to him that

I was planning to tell him tonight, it wouldn't be believed. So I did the only thing I knew I could do.

I turned, gathered up my things, and walked out of his apartment with my head held high. Inside, my heart was broken into so many pieces I knew it would never be put back together again.

About Summer Cooper

Thank you so much for reading. Without you, it wouldn't be possible for me to be a full-time author. I hope you enjoy reading my books as much as I do writing them.

Besides (obviously!) reading and writing, I also love cuddling my dogs, shouting at Alexa, being upside down (aka Yoga) and driving my family cray-cray!

Get in touch at
hello@summercooper.com
www.summercooper.com

Made in the USA
Columbia, SC
23 May 2025

58391824R00181